U0023544

Armageddon

There is a country in this world with two groups of people--one living aboveground and one underground. Long ago there was a defeat that led to the infiltration into the lives of underground people, which made for a bizarre legend for this country. And no one has ever truly seen them since. Fast forward a hundred years, there is finally the first person to return from the underground--the young Adolf.

Adolf: The first survivor from the underground, who was then promoted by the aboveground commanders, becoming leader in the development of the underground world.

Agneta: Working in education related departments and assigned as the person in charge of underground educational training with the purpose of unifying aboveground and underground people, making it easier to facilitate the conduct of government decrees and promotions.

Pina: Underground person, who was taken out of concentration camp because she saved Adolf after he fell into the underground world to promote underground people. Naturally passive. Submissive.

Sasha: Underground person. Promotes the use of underground people. Not attached to the past. Vehemently trying to melt into the aboveground society.

Helena: Underground person. Young girl promoting the use of underground people. Often homesick. A cry baby, who is often reprimanded by Agneta.

(Italics should be presented through pre-recorded audio)

(Light fade in, one spotlight on three women and another on one man. The man's spotlight is much dimmer than the women's. The three talk with the recording in perfect rhythm. The background music is like a heavy, complex Wagner. The women put out standard, proper poses and gestures. Look closely and you will notice that the three are so synchronized, even their breathing and blinking eyes are in unison before they speak. Adolf sucks on his lollipop.)

Sasha: Hello, everyone, I am Sasha.

Helena: I am Helena.

Pina: I am Pina.

Sasha: I am sure that all of you seated here will be very surprised to see how well we return aboveground and accept the changes in the mold of cultural society.

Helena: Like re-discovering the truth in the dark corridor.

Sasha: Is this what they called "enlightenment"?

Helena, Pina: Of course, is it not?

Helena: At first, we did not understand etiquette.

Pina: Aesthetics.

Sasha: And social norms.

Helena: I still remember when I first returned to the aboveground, "please," "thank you," "sorry," or "goodbye" were not included in my vocabulary. Therefore, when I was learning etiquette, I often mistook "goodbye" for "thank you."

(The pen in Helena's hand drops to the floor, Sasha pick it up for Helena)

Sasha: What should you say to me?

Helena: Thank you.

Sasha: I thought you still couldn't break your bad habit.

Pina: If Helena forgets again, then she should really be spanked.

Sasha: I think that's the meaning of education.

Pina: Being spanked?

(Adolf's section slowly lights up, Adolf bites on a lollipop and makes sounds with his mouth.)

Sasha: Of course not, in the process of accepting education for all, we have discovered that love is a key point in initial learning, which allows for tolerance, inculcation, and correction of what we have not yet learned. To respect oneself and therefore be respected is the compass of our education, and to quickly understand the necessity to comply with norms, as well as to maintain good personal standards and guidelines under the premise of our understanding. This is how we achieve the purpose of education.

Helena: It is therefore necessary to clarify frightening rumors of inhuman treatment.

Sasha: Otherwise we would be ungrateful to all the help and aid from Mr. Adolf.

(The three smile towards Adolf's direction. Adolf bites on a lollipop and makes sounds with his mouth.)

Pina: Rumors end with the wise.

Helena: We may stop here.

Sasha: Today we shall talk about art.

Pina: What is art?

Helena: If you ask me, art is the crystallization of human civilization.

Sasha: But more often, I believe it is the crystallization of the human soul.

Pina: Take fine arts for example.

Helena: Fine arts has an extensive history. It began with the advent of mankind.

Sasha: In primitive society, humans created drawings of animals and hunting on cave walls. With the development of civilization, the earliest words evolved from these pictures. Fine arts is a kind of spiritual product. It has always been associated with religion. With the progress in technology and the development of painting materials, artists continue to pursue more realistic depictions of objects, which then continues to expand the level of fine arts.

Helena: Of course, with the influence and status of fine arts in society along with the development of the theory behind it, fine arts itself is constantly changing.

Pina: Therefore, research has been done on fine arts history, the content of fine art pieces, the time and space of fine arts, and how the audience views these pieces of art. The styles of artwork and their historical ties are seen as the prerequisites for each piece of art, so before discussing art we must discuss the prerequisites.

Sasha: So, we believe whether it is classicism.

Pina: Or neoclassicism.

Helena: Realism.

Pina: Nonrealism.

Sasha: Reality.

Helena: Surrealism.

Sasha: Pastoral.

Sasha, Helena, Pina: Natural, abstract, dadaism, fauvism.

Sasha: They are all beautiful diamonds panned from the river of time; prying into the true meaning of life through each dazzling stone and its perfect refraction.

Helena: Art is not that far from us. Through education, through our own perceptions, we have found the touching moment that calls out to our souls in the midst of all those

colors, which completely inspires us to forever search for
beauty and the right attitude towards life.

Pina: I believe those seated here would like to know if the
"underground" has art or beauty or education.

Sasha: Unfortunately, no. So, we are very grateful, Mr. Adolf.

(Sasha, Helena, Pina all smile and wave towards Adolf's direction. Adolf bites on a lollipop and makes sounds with his mouth.)

Helena: And let us be able to regain the true meaning of life,
Miss Agneta.

(Agneta appears in a corner. Sasha, Helena, Pina all smile towards Agneta.)

Pina: As the highest authority of our education, Miss Agneta
always sets the best example, which benefit us, greatly.

Sasha: It is therefore necessary to clarify frightening rumors
of inhuman treatment.

Pina: Rumors end with the wise.

Helena: We may stop here.

Sasha: Today we shall talk about art. Still remember the first visit to Da Vinci's "Mona Lisa"(three of them smile like Mona Lisa.) that smile deeply engraved into my eyes, like luminous crystals making ripples as they are thrown in my heart; a poise and smile from hundreds of years ago encountered me today, as if the hundreds of years of existing was only for this brief rendezvous.

Helena: For me, the most impressive painting was "The Scream" by Edvard Munch (three of them make shouting actions) *those huge, empty eyes and mouth; as if they were deep holes sucking you in, sucking in everyone's uneasiness and panic only to extendedly spit it all back out. It is a silent scream, but can instantly become so noisy that is utterly unbearable.* (slowly dim lights)

Pina: "The Starry Night"; Van gogh's "The Starry Night", remember the first time I saw it, I shed many tears……

(lights dim, the three move to another section of the stage; and the recording starts to play again.)

Sasha: Hello, everyone. I am Sasha.

Helena: I am Helena.

Pina: I am Pina.

Sasha: I am sure that all of you seated here will be very surprised to see how well we return aboveground and accept the changes in the mold of cultural society.

Helena: Like re-discovering the truth in the dark corridor.

Sasha: Is this what they called "enlightenment"?

Helena, Pina: Of course, is it not?

Helena: At first, we did not understand etiquette.

Pina: Aesthetics.

Sasha: And social norms.

Helena: I still remember when I first returned to the aboveground, "please," "thank you," "sorry," or "goodbye" were not included in my vocabulary. Therefore, when I was learning etiquette, I often mistook "goodbye" for "thank you."

(The pen in Helena's hand drops to the floor, Sasha pick it up for Helena)

Sasha: What should you say to me?

Helena: Thank you.

Sasha: I thought you still couldn't quit your bad habit.

Pina: If Helena forgets again, then she should really be spanked.

Sasha: I think that's the meaning of education.

Pina: Being spanked?

(Adolf's section slowly lights up, Adolf bites on a lollipop and makes sounds with his mouth.)

Sasha: Of course not, in the process of accepting education for all, we have discovered that love is a key point in initial learning, which allows for tolerance, inculcation, and correction of what we have not yet learned. To respect oneself and therefore be respected is the compass of our education, and we quickly understand the necessity to comply with norms, as well as to maintain good personal standards and guidelines under the premise of our understanding. This is how we achieve the purpose of education.

Helena: It is therefore necessary to clarify frightening rumors of inhuman treatment.

Sasha: Otherwise we would be ungrateful to all the help and
aid from Mr. Adolf.

(The three smile towards Adolf's direction. Adolf bites on a lollipop and makes sounds with his mouth.)

Pina: Rumors end with the wise.

Helena: We may stop here.

Sasha: Today we shall talk about art.

Pina: What is art?

Helena: If you ask me, art is the crystallization of human
civilization.

Sasha: But more often, I believe it is the crystallization of the
human soul.

Pina: Take fine arts for example.

Helena: Fine arts has an extensive history. It began with the
advent of mankind.

Sasha: In primitive society, humans created drawings walls of
animals and hunting on cave. With the development of
civilization, the earliest words evolved from these pictures.
Fine arts is a kind of spiritual product. It has always been

associated with religion. With the progress in technology and the development of painting materials, artists continue to pursue more realistic depictions of objects, which then continues to expand the level of fine arts.

Helena: Of course, with the influence and status of fine arts in society along with the development of the theory behind it, fine arts itself is constantly changing.

Pina: Therefore, research has been done on fine arts history, the content of fine art pieces, the time and space of fine arts, and how the audience views these pieces of art. The styles of artwork and their historical ties are seen as the prerequisites for each piece of art, so before discussing art we must discuss the prerequisites.

Sasha: So, we believe whether it is classicism.

Pina: Or neoclassicism.

Helena: Realism.

Pina: Nonrealism.

Sasha: Reality.

Helena: Surrealism.

Sasha: Pastoral.

Sasha, Helena, Pina: Natural, abstract, dadaism, fauvism.

Sasha: They are all beautiful diamonds panned from the river of time; prying into the true meaning of life through each dazzling stone and its perfect refraction.

Helena: Art is not that far from us. Through education, through our own perceptions, we have found the touching moment that calls out to our souls in the midst of all those colors, which completely inspires us to forever search for beauty and the right attitude towards life.

Pina: I believe those seated here would like to know if the "underground" has art or beauty or education.

Sasha: Unfortunately, no. So, we are very grateful, Mr. Adolf.

(Sasha, Helena, Pina all smile and wave towards Adolf's direction. Adolf bites on a lollipop and makes sounds with his mouth.)

Helena: And let us be able to regain the true meaning of life, Miss Agneta.

(Agneta appears in a corner. Sasha, Helena, Pina all smile

towards Agneta.)

Pina: As the highest authority of our education, Miss Agneta always sets the best example, which benefit us, greatly.

Sasha: It is therefore necessary to clarify frightening rumors of inhuman treatment.

Pina: Rumors end with the wise.

Helena: We may stop here.

Sasha: Today we would like to talk about art. Still remember the first visit to Da Vinci's "Mona Lisa" (three of them smile like Mona Lisa.) *that smile deeply engraved into my eyes, like luminous crystals making ripples as they are thrown in my heart; a poise and smile from hundreds of years ago encountered me today, as if the sole purpose for existing hundreds of years was for this brief rendezvous.*

Helena: For me, the most impressive painting is "The Scream" by Edvard Munch (three of them make shouting actions) those huge, empty eyes and mouth; as if they were deep holes sucking you in, sucking in everyone's uneasiness and panic only to extendedly spit it all back out. It is a silent scream, but can instantly become so noisy that is utterly unbearable. (slowly dim lights)

Pina: "The Starry Night"; Van gogh's "The Starry Night", remember the first time I saw it, I shed many tears......

(lights dim, the three move to another section of the stage; and the recording starts to play again.)

Sasha: Hello, everyone. I am Sasha.

(Pina withdraws from the scene)

Helena: I am Helena.

Pina: I am Pina.

Pina: We are just exhibits. Pina? In Mother Earth's belly, I was never called this name. In the beginning when we were captured and brought to the aboveground world, we were only numbers. Everyone had to line up and wait for their number to be called, and then we were assigned to do labor in different places, or ......

Sasha: I am sure that all of you seated here will be very surprised to see how well we return aboveground and accept the changes in the mold of cultural society.

Helena: Like re-discovering the truth in the dark corridor.

Sasha: Is this what they called "enlightenment"?

Helena, Pina: Of course, are we not?

Helena: At first, we did not understand etiquette.

Pina: Aesthetics.

Sasha: And social norms.

Pina: At first, we did not need etiquette, aesthetics and social norms. We only needed to personally touch foreheads and make tweeting sounds. (Pina made some sounds like whales or dolphins, and immerses herself into making these sounds. She returns to her seat and continues to act according to the recording.)

Helena: I still remember when I first returned aboveground, the vocabulary in my head did not consist of "please," "thank you," "sorry," or "goodbye." So, when I was learning etiquette, I often thought "goodbye" was "thank you."

(The pen in Helena's hand drops to the floor, Sasha pick it up for Helena)

Sasha: What should you say to me?

Helena: Thank you.

(Helena freezes after receiving the pen, she then slowly moves away from the conversation block of three. The recording keeps playing.)

Helena: Please, thank you, sorry, please, thank you, sorry......
and goodbye. I will try my best to remember, I will try my best to remember. What is please? Please is to beg, so when I have to beg them to let me go, I need to say please spare me, please spare me, please spare me.

Agneta: Be elegant.

Helena: Be elegant in saying, "please spare me."

Agneta: Speak clearly, this is what we agreed upon.

Helena: Thank you, please spare me.

Agneta: No, it's "Sorry, please spare me." plus we also agreed that if a mistake is made, there should be a small reminder.

Helena: I know, sorry, please spare me.

Agneta: Open your mouth. (Helena looks at Agneta with pleading eyes ; Agneta uses a very friendly and gentle tone.) Open your mouth. (Agneta shoves a stick in Helena's mouth and forcibly stirs)

Agneta: You must speak clearly, your conversations must be logical, do you understand? (Agneta pulls out the stick and wipes it with her sole, Helena continues to retch and cough.) My little lady, what should you say now?

Helena: Thank you.

Agneta: Very good.

(Agneta resumes her states when she was first introduced. Helena returns to her seat and continues her actions.)

Sasha: I thought you still couldn't break your bad habit.

Pina: If Helena forgets again, then she should really be spanked.

Sasha: I think that's the meaning of education.

Pina: Being spanked?

(Adolf's section slowly lights up, Adolf bites on a lollipop and makes sounds with his mouth.)

Sasha: Of course not, in the process of accepting education for all, we have discovered that love is a key point in initial learning, which allows for tolerance, inculcation, and correction of what we have not yet learned. To respect oneself and therefore be respected is the compass of our education, and we quickly understand the necessity to comply with norms, as well as to maintain good personal standards and guidelines under the premise of our understanding. This is how we achieve the purpose of education.

Helena: It is therefore necessary to clarify frightening rumors of inhuman treatment.

Sasha: Otherwise we would be ungrateful to all the help and aid from Mr. Adolf.

(The three of them smile towards Adolf's direction. Adolf bites on a lollipop and makes sounds with his mouth.)

Pina: Rumors end with the wise.

Helena: We may stop here.

Sasha: Today we shall talk about art.

Pina: What is art?

Helena: If you ask me, art is the crystallization of human civilization.

Sasha: But more often, I believe it is the crystallization of the human soul.

Pina: Take fine arts for example.

Helena: Fine arts has an extensive history. It began with the advent of mankind.

Sasha: In primitive society, humans created drawings on cave walls of animals and hunting. With the development of civilization, the earliest words evolved from these pictures. Fine arts is a kind of spiritual product. It has always been associated with religion. With the progress in technology and the development of painting materials, artists continue to pursue more realistic depictions of objects, which then continues to expand the level of fine arts.

Helena: Of course, with the influence and status of fine arts in society along with the development of the theory behind it, fine arts itself is constantly changing.

Pina: Therefore, research has been done on fine arts history, the content of fine art pieces, the time and space of fine arts, and how the audience views these pieces of art. The styles of artwork and their historical ties are seen as the prerequisites for each piece of art, so before discussing art we must discuss the prerequisites.

Sasha: So, we believe whether it is classicism.

Pina: Or neoclassicism.

Helena: Realism.

Pina: Nonrealism.

Sasha: Reality.

Helena: Surrealism.

Sasha: Pastoral.

Sasha, Helena, Pina: Natural, abstract, dadaism, fauvism.

Sasha: They are all beautiful diamonds panned from the river of time; prying into the true meaning of life through each dazzling stone and its perfect refraction.

Helena: Art is not that far from us. Through education, through our own perceptions, we have found the touching moment that calls out to our souls in the midst of all those colors, which completely inspires us to forever search for beauty and the right attitude towards life.

Pina: I believe those seated here would like to know if the "underground" has art or beauty or education.

Sasha: Unfortunately, no. So, we are very grateful to Mr. Adolf.

(Sasha, Helena, Pina all smile and wave towards Adolf's direction. Adolf bites on a lollipop and makes sounds with his mouth.)

Helena: And to Miss Agneta, who helps us recollect the truth in life.

(Agneta appears in a corner. Sasha, Helena, Pina all smile towards Agneta.)

Pina: As the highest authority of our education, Miss Agneta always sets the best example, which benefit us, greatly.

Sasha: It is therefore necessary to clarify frightening rumors of inhuman treatment.

Pina: Rumors end with the wise.

Helena: We may stop here.

Sasha: Today we shall talk about art. Still remember the first visit to Da Vinci's "Mona Lisa" (three of them smile like Mona Lisa.) *that smile deeply engraved into my eyes, like luminous crystals making ripples as they are thrown in my heart; a poise and smile from hundreds of years ago encountered me today, as if the sole purpose for existing hundreds of years was for this brief rendezvous.*

Helena: For me, the most impressive painting was "The Scream" by Edvard Munch (three of them make shouting actions) *those huge, empty eyes and mouth; as if they were deep holes sucking you in, sucking in everyone's uneasiness and panic only to extendedly spit it all back out. It is a silent scream, but can instantly become so noisy that is utterly unbearable.* (slowly dim lights)

Pina: "The Starry Night"; Van gogh's "The Starry Night", remember the first time I saw it, I shed many tears......
(Pina leaves again)

Pina: "The Starry Night"; Van gogh's "The Starry Night", remember the first time I saw it, I shed many tears, a sheet of darkness and depth rotating in the quiet night sky; sparkle after sparkle of bright specks light up the rotating darkness, which reminds me of long tunnels, looking onward on both sides of the tunnel there is a dim light in front of homes, and from time to time there is an echo that sounds through.

(Lights dim)

(Recording continues after lights go up. Only Sasha is left to do the actions while talking with Helena. Helena sits quietly on the side and plays with her skirt, both continuously repeating their conversation.)

Sasha: Helena, you should listen to teacher Agneta.

Helena: What if I'd rather be beaten to death.

Sasha: Then you'd better not come asking me to save you......

(Another section is lit. Commander and Agneta)

Commander: The underground exploration case is still in progress, but the roar of criticism from the people has become so loud; Agneta, I think as the highest authority of our education, you should personally teach these uncivilized underground people, so they may in the shortest time be able to perform acts of ceremony.

Agneta: (looks reluctant) I know; but Prime Minister, I heard they were aggressive, that and my concerned about their ability to communicate have left me full of doubt.

Commander: Agneta, I never thought you would be startled by the exaggerated media coverage.

Agneta: Yes.

Commander: If they are indeed beasts, then educate them as so.

Agneta: Educate them as beasts?

Commander: (gives Agneta a stick) I order you to give me the best results in the shortest time, no matter what kind of educational means you use. Swearing on the honor of the society aboveground; Adolf has done a good job about this.

Agneta: Swearing on the superior blood of the society aboveground, …… I will do better than Adolf.

(Agneta breaks into Sasha and Helena's section and begins to beat Helena, Sasha still repeats "Helena, you should listen to teacher Agneta." Helena begins to run away in pain, but Agneta goes in hot pursuit.)

Sasha: Now are the first few days after being selected by Mr. Adolf. Mr. Adolf tells us that, to be the exhibits from underground, we have great potential and depth, so the aboveground government is putting us through so much educating and etiquette training, to show that underground people still withhold manners and rituals even aboveground.

Helena, you should listen to teacher Agneta.

Agneta: I have no right to express my sympathy, all my duties are to obey orders. Showing loyalty and obedience is everything. Loyalty is virtue, trust me!

Sasha: Miss Agneta hates it when we disobey. She's always a bit neurotic. She screams when we squirm, because she thinks we will attack her...... Helena, you should listen to Miss Agneta.

Agneta: I am always devout and devoted to implementing tasks, and I've always been proud of belonging to the noble race of the society aboveground. I feel its value......

Sasha: Helena is my little attendant, but she is just too lazy, (looks at Helena and Agneta) too lazy; hence why teacher Agneta often beats her so harshly, teacher Agneta also beats me sometimes, (secretly) you know, only those specific few days. Helena, you should listen to teacher Agneta.

Agneta: I have no right to express sympathy, all my duties are to just obey orders. To be loyal and obedient is everything. Loyalty is an important character, trust me!

Sasha: In the beginning teacher Agneta never hit anyone, so we improved so slowly; but ever since Mr. Adolf intervened in our educational classes, Miss Agneta has now become anxious; So she learned how to use the stick and is getting better and better, the rate we're improving has become faster.

(Helena fled to Sasha's side.)

Helena: Sasha, I beg of you to help me.

Sasha, Helena: (Pause) Beasts don't have love, beasts don't have rules; we use whips, we use jagged love. So wailing is the best response to learning.

(Sasha and Pina look at each other for a moment and quickly break eye contact.)

Adolf: This is Pina.

(Sasha leaves her seat, but stays wandering around. Pina joins Helena's movements.)

Sasha: Mr. Adolf.

Adolf: Your new partner.

Sasha: Mr. Adolf, do you think I am qualified to be one of the aboveground people?

Adolf: I need you to encourage each other.

Sasha: Mr. Adolf, is this elegant enough?

Agneta: Adolf, you keep bringing people here at random, don't you worry about training period and demonstration deadlines?

Adolf: Since we have an expert of education here, Agneta. One more student should be ok

Sasha: Mr. Adolf, You should feel satisfied to have me. I won't let you down.

Agneta: Adolf, are you trying to give me a hard time?

Adolf: Agneta, Agneta, first of all, this demonstration program is designed by both the Department of Underground Development and the Ministry of Education; second of all, there are only two people now for the demonstration. Prime Minister does not think it is enough. Or would you prefer that I convey to the Prime Minister a message saying, "Agneta's workload is too much, I'm afraid she can't handle it."

Agneta: No need to do that, as an expert in education, I do not
  have this problem.

Adolf: Then I wish you well, Agneta.

(Adolf left the stage, Agneta stares at Adolf bitterly.)

Sasha: That was the last good old day--the day when Pina
  arrived.

(Air raid alarm, everyone is terrified and starts their actions,
something starts to go wrong with the recording, the three
stutter and fumble through attempts to fill in missing parts of
the recording. Anita begins to recite instructions, faster and
faster, more and more chaotic, until the three exhaustingly
fall to the ground.)

Agneta: Get up! Get up! Don't make me tie a rocket to your
  bottoms.

(The three gasp on the floor. They try to get up, but fail and
fall down.)

Agneta: Get up! (Agneta beats Sasha, who has fallen on the
  ground, Sasha gets up and begins to run around the
  whole stage while doing her ritual actions, then collapses

on the ground again. In follows Pina and Helena; the three run around the stage and fall down. Agneta keeps beating and chasing after them. The three cry for mercy and screams words like, "I can't do it.")

Adolf: Agneta your ways of educating are about to fail, other than beating them up like scurrying sows, you haven't taught them anything.

Agneta: Get up! Before they become educated candidates, they must first learn to be afraid of pain. Get up! Sows!

Adolf: I hope your education compass is correct, otherwise Prime Minister will be very disappointed.

Agneta: Needless to say, I will train up the best underground protocol for the Prime Minister, because I am a superior member of the aboveground society! (She fumbles) Get up, you!

Adolf: Hahaha, I will report to the Prime Minister that you are most strict with manners and conduct.

Agneta: You bastard, this is not my responsibility alone! If I suffer, you will too! Maybe I'm not your only enemy, but now I am your only ally! You better remember this. Get up! Sows.

(A cold Adolf walks towards the women and uses brute force to drag their representation dolls one by one together in one place. He mutters as he drags. The women gather together scared and miserable.")

Adolf: To allow underground people to be "aboveground-nized" we must first provide a strong and sound environment, then work on educating them individually. Education is the most important issue, because they have to recognize our strength in culture, economy and politics in order to be willing to surrender into our society. We have no choice but to begin with education. You make one of them driven by in fear, and the rest of them will learn to awe. If she does not understand fear and pain and such, then how do you produce respect from her?

Agneta: Education is important, so the next cabinet prime minister should be served by the Minister of Education.

Adolf: I'm sick of this war of words. Since you are my only

ally, I have done my best to assist you, the rest is up to you.

Agneta: Do not think I will be the least bit grateful of your miniscule amount of help.

Adolf: 12 days from now, the Prime Minister will need the "First Endeavor." To share with the other gentlemen. Since this is inconvenient for me to teach…… it's all yours.

(Adolf goes off stage.)

Agneta: Adolf! Don't go, you bastard. (Looks at the three) Fine, this is the first day…… we still have 11 days to go.

(Lights dim)

(lights slowly brighten, the three frightened women and Agneta stand on stage in a graceful manner.)

Agneta: Let me know who is best suited to accompany the Prime Minister.

Sasha: Miss Agneta, maybe Pina is the one, she has a plump figure! I'm sure the Prime Minister will like her.

Pina: Miss Agneta, am i a little too plump?

Agneta: Stupid Helena is most definitely not suitable for accompanying the Prime Minister, Pina has certainly gained some weight, Sasha … turn around.

Sasha: Miss Agneta, I think I might be too skinny?

Agneta: (Beats Sasha with a stick) Turn around. (Helena turns around) It seems like the Prime Minister will be very satisfied with you, you're the one.

Sasha: Miss Agneta, don't do it, Please?

Agneta: This is not up to you or me to decide! It's your own fault your despicably dirty bodies are unable to contract AIDS, please do your best to service the Prime Minister and the other gentlemen.

Sasha: Mr. Adolf will be there, too?

Agneta: Maybe.

Sasha: I beg of you, please don't do this! Please don't make me do such things.

Agneta: You have no right to refuse. (pause) Perhaps I will ask Mr. Adolf to the scene to monitor whether you have indeed carried out this task.

Sasha: (almost faints) Miss Agneta, (Helena and Pina approach to catch Sasha from fainting)

Helena: Sister, sister, are you okay?

Sasha: (pause) Miss Agneta, Helena is still a virgin! I believe the Prime Minister and the other gentlemen will enjoy her very much.

Helena: Sasha?

Agneta: Oh, is that so?

Sasha: Yes, Miss Agneta, Helena she is purer than the rest of us.

Helena: Miss Agneta! I beg you, please spare me.

Agneta: We must ask for perfection. The three of you will sooner or later be summoned by the Prime Minister and the other gentlemen, we might as well let the three of you go together now and save you all from selling each other out. (the three of them are terrified) go and present a little bit of usefulness for the aboveground society.

(Agneta exits with the three women, Helena and Sasha stops after awhile; lights around Sasha and Helena, lights down for the other sections.)

Helena: Dear sister Sasha, why are you setting me up?

Sasha: Helena, have you ever liked anyone?

Helena: ...... yes.

Sasha: Then you should know how mournful it is to be humiliated by someone else in front of the person you love.

Helena: Mr. Adolf?

Sasha: Yes.

Helena: Sister Sasha, Mr. Adolf doesn't care about any of us.

Sasha: No, as long as I keep working hard and improving myself, one day Mr. Adolf will affirm and sincerely accept me.

Helena: Dear sister, you are willing to sell me out just for that sliver of hope? We are on the same side, aren't we?

Sasha: Of course we are together; so wait for me to connect with Mr. Adolf, and I will let you live a comfortable life aboveground just like me, okay?

Helena: You want to sacrifice me for that slight chance?...... Sacrifice my first time?

Sasha: Your first time? Who do you think you are? The princess waiting for the prince in the castle? Or sleep beauty? Don't be silly! We all know we're worthless, and since we cannot know which gentlemen will end up doing us … we might as well give ourselves to the Prime Minister; (pause) if you don't say anything then leave with Miss Agneta, there's no need to drag me and Pina down. The only place you can be of some use, you come out useless. (Helena cries, Sasha suddenly becomes softer) Don't cry, (pressing on her heart) The first time will hurt more, after that everything will be fine…… after that everything will be fine.

(Lights dim)

(Lights on, when the lights come back on, six men are behind Helena moving happily, Helena lies on a turning table.)

Helena: We are women of good manners. We hang manners on our eyes, by our mouths. We respect logic. We have gratitude towards intellectual conversations. We have our own salvation through speculation.

(Helena shows a very frightened expression and spasms, lights dim. When lights return, the Prime Minister and other gentlemen are enjoying the services of Helena and Sasha.)

Prime Minister: Whao! Not bad, not bad.

A: Agneta says yours is a virgin!

Prime Minister: Oh! How come she doesn't seem like one at all?

(both laugh)

A: The Prime Minister is asking why you don't seem like a virgin at all.

Helena: Because I must service the Prime Minister well.

A: Because you must service the Prime Minister well! Haha!

Prime Minister: Then you must do it good.

A: Can she?

Prime Minister: It doesn't look like it, you must do it good!

A: Yes, yes, yes! Prime Minister, I will! I will perform well. (forcibly and rudely attacks Sasha.) Let me take care of this one first.

Prime Minister: Quickly, quickly, quickly, I'm waiting here for you to take over.

(Adolf enters)

Adolf: Prime Minister, gentlemen, good evening.

Prime Minister: Oh, our fresh trooper is here.

A: Adolf, hurry and help Prime Minister! He is awfully busy over there.

Sasha: Mr. Adolf, you ......

A: (Puts the dildo back into Sasha's mouth) Keep going, don't be wanting to change now that you see the young one...... he's no match for my skills

Prime Minister: You're pretty good, you little rascal! Then I can't lose to you either. (The cabinet Prime Minister turn Helena over and enters from behind, Helena screams.) Yes! Yes! This one is a virgin, no doubt. There is a lot of enjoyment packed in here.

A: Prime Minister can really develop virgin territory. Always executing with full vigor and urgency.

Prime Minister: Virgin territory. (Looks down at his crotch) But surely there are still some filthiness. Adolf, progress report.

Adolf: (a little worried) those two women …

Prime Minister: Don't mind them, go ahead and speak.

Adolf: Yes. The militia campaign, which began last week, processed about 250,000 people, next we will dispose based on pupil and hair color.

Prime Minister: Still too slow. What about the names?

Adolf: For convenience, we have added names to the original underground people who were originally assigned numbers, this will help calm the condemning voices against foreign governments. We can also eliminate by letters; the only concern is rationalizing the massacre.

A: We need no reason to massacre underground people.

Prime Minister: Today it's H's turn, go go go, Adolf, throw everyone with an H in their names into the fire or gas chamber. Helena, you too, you too. Hahaha.

Helena: Prime Minister, please spare me!

Sasha: Helena!

A: Be obedient and do as you should.

(Cabinet Prime Minister leaves from Helena's side, and pulls Helena towards the door with one hand, Helena continues to beg for mercy.)

Adolf: Prime Minister ...... !

Prime Minister: Shhh!

Helena: Prime Minister, I beg of you! Please don't send me to the gas chamber!

Prime Minister: Then what should you do?

(Helena quietly turns, sticks her bottom up high, and pulls up her skirt.)

Helena: We are women of good manners. We hang manners on

our eyes, by our mouths. We respect logic. We have gratitude towards intellectual conversations. We have our own salvation through speculation.

Prime Minister: Very good, very good! Adolf, you and Agneta have done well teaching these sows; now I want to see them continuously appearing on TV putting on a gentle and virtuous look so we may block the talk that we are tormenting and killing underground people, and to block those against the development of underground society.

A: If even we do so, they can't stop us. (after speaking, plugs his penis deep in Sasha's mouth, Sasha can't help but gag) No fun. (Prime Minister and A let out a big laugh)

Adolf: (takes out a handkerchief and gives it to Sasha) Wipe yourself clean.

Sasha: (gratefully) Mr. Adolf, thank you.

A: Really, a gentleman here makes us look like wolves and tigers and leopards. Prime Minister: Adolf, you may leave.

Adolf: Yes, I wish you both have much fun.

(Adolf exits)

A: What about the other little sow?

Prime Minister: Is she with the others in another room?

A: I'll go find them.

Prime Minister: See what games they're playing there.

(Prime Minister and A leave Sasha and Helena, Helena quietly weeps as Sasha wrings the handkerchief; lights slowly dim)

(Recording enters, lights slowly enter; Adolf appears on stage.)

Adolf: There's a warmth in rationality, so you bake at a low heat to prevent any damages; and occasionally using high heat. Women in clear frames accept the tremors of rationale. Wave after wave it enters their bodies into their deepest education. Come, come, come, as long as they learn to smile and nod, logic and sex are on them.

(Agneta leads the three women on stage, the three women are wearing prison uniforms.)

Agneta: Smile! Learn to smile.

Helena: Miss Agneta, we are really so sleepy.

Agneta: I do not need to hear your complaint right now.

Helena: I'm really so tired.

Adolf: I don't think this is the time to express personal opinions.

Sasha: Helena, please stop complaining, we are all the same.

Agneta: Everyone, shut up.

Sasha: Miss Agneta, I am…….

Agneta: (hysterical) Talk back! I do not need to hear you all talk back!

Adolf: Agneta, what happened to your education with love?

Agneta: My education? For this pitiful ones? What kind of education do you want from me? They are lowly and dangerous, this is why they are locked up in a concentration camp. Go inside! (Agneta points to shower room, the three women begin to squirm restlessly.)

Sasha: Go inside?

Agneta: Go inside!

Pina: Go inside?

Helena: I beg of you! Dear Miss Agneta! Please don't!

Sasha: Where is that?

Helena: Is that the place the gentlemen were tell us about?

Sasha: It's just like the rumors, it's just like the rumors!

Pina: Why should we be destroyed?

Adolf: Agneta, they are rejecting your order.

Agneta: Go inside!

Adolf: (contemptuously) Agneta, they want to revolt against you.

Agneta: (on the verge of insanity, pushes and beats the three
women) Go inside!!

(Three women are pushed by Agneta, Sasha and Pina
escape in different directions, Helena is pushed into the
shower room.)

Agneta: Adolf, I hate these underground women. They make me
physically feel hatred and disgust, I feel sick to my stomach
each time I look at their low life faces. Plus, they love
hugging in a group, protecting each other! Because God has
abandoned them, that's why they can't get aids, even God
disdains from punishing them, allowing them to engage in
wanton and wicked underground debauchery.

(lights change, three women are in the light, the extremely
frightened women let out cried of desperation, Adolf and
Agneta stay in their positions.)

Pina: When removing clothes, do so in a most calm atmosphere
as possible. Children usually cry, because taking off clothes
in this unaccustomed manner was undeniably inscrutable.
However, the crying commonly stopped after mothers or

members of the aboveground collection squad of corpses comforted the children. They would then obediently enter the gas chambers with their toys and would sometimes still be horsing around, unaware of what was to instored. Hundreds of boys and girls, in the prime of their youths, entered the gas chambers to their deaths in a similar fashion, without a hint of doubt. Outside, the fruit trees were in full bloom. So much life concurring with so much death. After the poisoning, other underground people were forced to carry corpses to trucks, which transferred them onto a temporary railway line, which then disposed of the bodies in a vast pit.

Sasha: Someone is screaming, the aboveground people shout, "Hurry up......" The underground people were ordered to take off their clothes, then forced to walk into a further room in the compound, being told they were to shower there, can you imagine what the children's families were about to encounter? They were thinking...... they did not know what to do. They began scratching the walls with their nails, crying and screaming until the gas began to take effect. After it was all over, they opened the door. The people I saw enter the chamber an hour ago were now all standing straight, some became black and blue from the poisonous gas, nowhere to run, they were all dead.

Helena: The poison gas begins to take effect after three to fifteen minutes. After a period of time the interval of gas discharge should be shortened. But to deal with twelve thousand underground people a day, the dosage was increased. A few minutes is enough to kill a newborn baby; when they were dragged out, some entire bodies turned into an eerie fluorescent blue. But sometimes when the gas chambers were opened, a few were not dead yet, some had a higher tolerance for the poisonous gas. Sometimes some little underground people had a higher tolerance than adults to rat poisoning gas.

(Silence)

Sasha, Helena, Pina: Those that did not die--including children--were also thrown in the incinerator along with the corpses!!

(Sasha and Pina finished speaking and rushed into the shower room as if they were sucked in, the frightened three scurried around in a small space and screamed until Adolf raised his hands in silence)

Adolf: Turn it on.

(Water poured out of the showerhead, the three were stunned)

Adolf, Agneta: Everyone respects me, I am an important figure.

(lights change, the three women leave the shower room towards imaginary underground world, water continues to flow from the showerhead, Adolf appears on stage.)

Adolf: We also let the concentration camps be infected with staphylococci, gas-borne astragalus, tetanus and mixed cultivations of several pathogenic bacteria, the purpose being to study the therapeutic effects of sulfonamides. We did not carry out any truly responsible monitoring, resulting in the lower parts of the prisoners' legs getting infected without their knowledge. When a few survivors appeared to heal with scars, the wound would often but deeply cut open until the bones exposed. In addition to the implanting bacteria into the wound tissues, there would also often be wood chips and glass slag inserted. The legs of the subject quickly began to suppurate. In order to observe the development of the situation, the victims would not be given any treatment, they were often died from extreme pain...... each series of experiments repeated at least six times, using six to ten young women - usually choosing the most beautiful. And also performing permanent sterilization surgery on the underground people, with a feasible way via sufficient amounts of radiation, and then onto castrations, which produced a series of related consequences. A large number of X-rays destroys the ovarian or testicular endocrine capacity...... but because surrounding tissue with lead plates was impossible, so we had to acknowledge a tricky problem that these organs would be destroyed and consequently was followed by the effects of so-called "side effects" of X-rays. Excessive exposure to radiation over following few days or few weeks led to burns on exposed skin. For example, a very feasible way is to put the subject in front of a counter, let them stand there for about three minutes, answer some questions, or fill out forms. The clerk behind the counter can press the button to start the radiation instrument, so that two X-ray tube shot the ray of radiation at the same time, this is because the radiation must also be from both sides. Through these methods, using dual-channel radiation instruments, 150 to 200 people could be sterilization per day, if there are twenty sets of such equipment, three thousand to four thousand people could be done per day...... a few weeks or a few months later, even if those people discovered they were sterilized, it would still be pretty irrelevant.

(In the midst of underground world they imagine, the three people hug in different positions to the flow of music, softly humming along with irregular sounds of the song "Home" until the music endends, as light dims; the showerhead continued to flow until the lights go up for the next scene.)

(Lights on, Adolf is organizing files, Agneta enters.)

Agneta: Congratulations on our first 100 shows and television appearances.

Adolf: (doesn't even look up) Hm.

Agneta: Are there a lot of files that need organizing?

Adolf: (still organizing files) Yes.

Agneta: What are you busy doing?

Adolf: Aftermath.

Agneta: Aftermath? I thought you'd be swamped with developing underground energy; Prime Minister probably has you accountable for a not so light workload?

Adolf: (finally looks up) Agneta, why exactly have you come?

Agneta: Nothing really, I came especially to see how you were doing.

Adolf: A straightforward person does not resort to insinuations.

Agneta: Adolf, you are always this impervious! I am here to see if Prime Minister is about to have you deal with the underground protocol.

Adolf: No.

Agneta: No, is to say that since more than a month ago activities showcasing underground people have been completely suspended?

Adolf: Yes.

Agneta: Don't they need to use the showcase to bleach the entire underground development program?

Adolf: Showcasing underground people has already been busted, people have lost interest in them.

Agneta: So. this whole month or so you haven't met with Prime Minister.

Adolf: Only for routine development progress reports.

Agneta: So, the Prime Minister has not summoned them again to "service" him and the other gentlemen.

Adolf: No.

Agneta: So, the underground boom is over?

Adolf: I think so.

Agneta: There are more and more people who criticize the development of the underground world?

Adolf: Agneta, are you not an educator? Then how come you

have flipped to being like a student, asking questions like crazy.

Agneta: You're not worried about losing power after the boom is over?

Adolf: All I have to do is live, nothing else.

Agneta: Adolf, Adolf, you are always this impervious. (Agneta turns around to leave) No wonder you were able to become the killer demon in the underground that everyone was talking about.

(Agneta goes down; Adolf stops what he's doing, falls into an ambiguous mood. Pina appears inside Adolf's room, Sasha is walking non-stop around the four corners of the room.)

Pina: Mr. Adolf, you are looking of me?

Adolf: Mhmm, how are you all doing lately?

Pina: Thanks to you, we're doing relatively well, we've passed
    some leisurely days.

Adolf: Helena is still so jumpy?

Pina: (Discreetly) Helena is not used to servicing the gentlemen.

Adolf: So you and Sasha are used to it?

Pina: If we have no choice, we can only get used to it.

Adolf: Many things come with no right to choose.

Pina: Yes.

Adolf: (pause) Then how do you feel, about you and Sasha?

Pina: You know she totally admires Mr. Adolf.

Adolf: Even after the way I treat you all?

(the following Sasha lines Pina also says them, but in an extremely low volume.)

Sasha: Mr. Adolf, I totally admire your meticulousness; no matter how you treat me, I know that comes from a helplessness of following orders from above.

Adolf: Or when she was in the middle of servicing the gentlemen and saw me?

Sasha: I know you are unable to reverse the situation, but you use your meticulous ways to love me...... us, and not like the typical gentleman out to use us, enjoy us. Mr. Adolf, my body can be shared with any gentleman, but the pureness of my heart only allows you to enter.

Adolf: Rats can only be with rats, wolves can only be with wolves, foxes can only be with foxes, geese can only mate with other geese, as to maintain the purity of the species. Absolutely no cat will fall in love with a rat, the people aboveground have the same obligation.

Sasha: Why?

Pina: Mr. Adolf, why?

Adolf: In order to protect the blood and purity.

Pina: Mr. Adolf, do you really think so?

Adolf: As the highest leader in the development of the underground world, I never doubt anything I have said.

Pina: What you've said? What about the Prime Minister?

Adolf: That question is beyond your limits.

Pina: I'm very sorry.

(silence, Sasha exits.)

Adolf: Do you believe in salvation?

Pina: What?

Adolf:Do you have hatred? For the aboveground society?

Pina: Mr. Adolf, if we have no other choice, then what can we do with our hatred?

Adolf: Revenge?

Pina: That is something all of us do not dare to imagine, how can we be enemies of the whole aboveground society?

Adolf: So you choose to be at the mercy of others? Would it be, actually, that the fight of the underground people allows you to still safely live underground?

Pina: But we have been dug up from the underground, have we not?

Adolf: (emotional) Why did you not resist when you were dug up?!

Pina: Death, so we can only live with together with death.

Adolf: Even now?

Pina: Even now, I still feel death breathing by my ear.

Adolf: And I am the farmer that spreads the seeds of death.

Pina: You have been most responsible.

Adolf: Yes, I am most responsible.

Pina: (laughs) Everyone says, "There is no God in the concentration camps, because it is so terrifying here that even God has decided not to come."

Adolf: Seems like fulfilling my duties has won me an unprecedented victory.

Pina: Yes.

(Silence)

Adolf: Sasha hates you? Because I often summon you here?

Pina: I try my best to make her not hate me.

Adolf: It must be very difficult?

Pina: Because we only have each other left.

Adolf: Pina, how can you be so calm?

Pina: When I could have protested I didn't speak up, now I can only accept.

Adolf: Any situation, you can accept?

Pina: There's nothing worse; I stayed in a concentration camp, I've seen a son beat his father to death over a loaf of bread. I've seen people stampede others to death just to dodge a bullet. There's not much difference between being alive and dead.

Adolf: It seems that the concentration camps are run very well.

Pina: Yes.

(long pause)

Adolf: If I did not find you?

Pina: Then I would probably be sleeping for a long time underground with my mother right now.

Adolf: But I could only bring the three of you out with me.

Pina: I know, Mr. Adolf has already violated the rules of your work.

Adolf: Now with the way you are living, will you hate me?

Pina: No, I can only focus on the moment, I do not have the ability to think about the past or the future.

Adolf: Pina, you hate me, don't you?

Pina: Mr. Adolf, I will only think about what work I must do an hour from now, love and hate are not things I can control……

Adolf: Mr. Adolf? Fine, I order you to answer me! Go ahead, hate me.

Pina: I hate you, I can't wait to kill and dismember you, then hang your head high on a flagpole for all the underground people to see.

(long pause)

Adolf: This way, will your hatred disperse?

Pina: No.

(silence)

Pina: I know this is your job, you are only executing faithfully; there are no bad people in this world, only different perspectives is all.

Adolf: But you hate me?

Pina: Yes.

(long pause)

Adolf: So all the underground people have cast me aside?

Pina: Correct, Mr. Adolf surely will not be able to get any
forgiveness from the underground people.

Adolf: Even Sasha?

Pina: I believe deep in her heart, she is also hating you.

(long pause)

Adolf: Forever impossible to be forgiven?

Pina: Forever, but forever doesn't mean anything.

Adolf: Go back then.

Pina: Yes.

(Pina turns around and leaves)

Adolf: What if you are allowed back underground?

Pina: Mr. Adolf, if a fish is set free in a pond of blood can it still
live?

Adolf: So you do not wish to go back?

Pina: I cannot go back.

Adolf: go back……

Pina:…… also impossible to forgive.

(pause)

Adolf: I know.

Pina: Then I'm going back now.

Adolf: But you know this is all dictated by work, right?

Pina: I completely understand.

(pause)

Adolf: You and your family saved me when I fell into the hole.

Pina: Yes.

Adolf: Do you regret it now?

Pina: A little; but if I did not save you, the same thing would have happened; at least I'm grateful it's you.

Adolf: What do you mean by that?

Pina: You are always just precisely executing your tasks, you don't overly torture people.

Adolf: So I am sort of forgiven, just a little bit.

Pina: Maybe one hundred thousandth of a percent (pause) Mr. Adolf, I'm leaving now.

(Pina turns around and leaves)

Adolf: Thank you.

Pina: (doesn't turn head) No problem.

(Pina exits; Adolf stays on stage, lights slowly dim.)

(In a semi-bright light, the three women pace and smoke non-stop in a small, cold room, until the three simultaneously put out their cigarettes; Helena walks towards a window and stares endlessly outside, Pina is reading on the side while she rolls roses.)

Sasha: Helena, what are you looking at?

Helena: We haven't been in any showcases or TV shows for two months now.

Sasha: This is good, we don't have to memorize art history or squeeze out a smiling face.

Helena: The gentlemen have not come for a long time either.

Sasha: You hope for them to come?

Helena: Of course not.

Sasha: (cold laugh) But the way you're talking, it sounds like you are really hoping for them to come; next time the gentlemen come, I will tell them you were really looking forward to them coming, you wait for them by the window every day.

Helena: (appalled) No; dear sister Sasha, please do not tell them that, otherwise……

Sasha: Otherwise, what?

Helena: Otherwise they will carve the date on my body again.

Pina: Helena, why don't you come and sit with me?

Sasha: Pina, we are having a lovely talk.

(Sasha and Pina look at each other briefly, Pina then lowers her head to continue reading.)

Helena: (looking toward the window, whispering) It's okay, I want to look outside.

Sasha: Helena, you could read like Pina; See, Pina can be closer with Mr. Adolf because she reads so much, reading is a good thing.

Helena: I don't like it, reading makes me think of Miss Agneta's stick…… Miss Agneta hasn't come for a long time, (pause) Mr. Adolf, too. Oh right, Pina, what did Mr. Adolf want last time he called you to his office?

Pina: Nothing, just asked about some things.

Helena: What did you do?

Pina: Boring trivial stuff, nothing worth saying.

(Sasha pushes herself up from her chair, she pretends to pull the chair, she has a book in one hand, half throwing and half shoving it into Helena's lap.)

Sasha: Big mouth! Don't ask things others don't want to talk about.

Helena: Mhmm.

Sasha: Mouths talk about joys and sorrows, which in fact, is a privilege.

Pina: (pleading) Sasha.

Helena: I don't need privileges, I just want to go back.

Sasha: Go back? Go back to where?

Helena: Underground. I really want to eat Mom's roasted hamster.

Sasha: Disgusting! Do you see any aboveground people eating this dish? It's barbaric.

Helena: But it's really delicious. Maybe because they've just never had it before. Let's invite them to try some, maybe the aboveground people will fall crazy in love with roasted hamster.

Sasha: I really can't believe that you have been educated for so long and can still say such things; barbaric, this is a show of barbarism.

Pina: Rosemary white snails are also pretty good!

Helena: Oh! Only on birthdays can we enjoy rosemary white snails; every year when Mom cooks this, the fragrance fills the air for two or three hundred meters. Everyone usually brings a gift in exchange for a snail.

Pina: Eating snails brings good luck to underground people.

(pause)

Helena: We must not have eaten enough. I miss Mom so much.

Sasha: Helena, you are so weak, it's annoying!

Pina: We all miss home.

Sasha: We all know that it is not a place for living.

Pina: Winters are so cold it feels as though our bones will be frozen, so we always huddle around the stove running and jumping.

Helena: We were so happy then.

Sasha: Shut up!

(silence)

Pina: "The Starry Night," Van Gogh's "The Starry Night," remember the first time I saw it, I shed many tears, a sheet of darkness and depth rotating in the quiet night sky; sparkle after sparkle of bright specks light up the rotating darkness, which reminds me of long tunnels, looking onward on both sides of the tunnel there is a dim light in front of homes, and from time to time there is an echo that sounds through. The streaks in the night sky are like the sounds and smells of the underground.

Helena: How can you not miss home?

Pina: Do you remember? Do you remember? Before leaving the sewer for the last time, our past was collapsing. We were forced out of our mother's warm womb. That's where I lived for decades. For decades, that's where I lived! Home! Home!

Sasha: So what? Beautiful houses are with no use. Who has the right to do this? A printed announcement, a force of power, yanking us out of the underground without looking at our roots, without listening to our grieving cries.

Helena: My small small room had a window, at night you could hear the sounds of bugs crawling by. I still remember a summer that was particularly hot, there were so many so many little flying insects, my lights made them drill through the screen and fly into my room, tiny black specks covered my white walls, this made me run out of my room with panic looking for my mother to save me......

(long pause, Sasha, with great force, throws her book on the ground)

Sasha: Helena! It's too dark, turn the light up.

(Helena paused for a moment, then turned up the lights)

Sasha: You're daydreaming again, daydreams won't make your days any better. Plus, it's so great to have power and running water, no need to worry about exploding gas lamps and smelling like well water after a shower.

Pina: It's all coming back to me.

Sasha: Pina, we should look forward, we are now part of the aboveground society; the most practical thing to do is to think about how to be a better aboveground person. (pause) Helena is like a little sister to me, how can I let her immerse herself back in the shadow of the past?

Pina: Now we are living in darkness.

Helena: The lights aren't bright enough?

Sasha: Sweet Helena, that is a silly metaphor that you don't need to understand; we just need to fulfill our responsibilities and display the most elegant side of underground people willing to be educated, that's enough, that's our job.

Pina: Even if millions of underground people have died already.

(Helena lets out a short cry, then looks frightened.)

Helena: "Today it's H's turn, go go go, Adolf, throw everyone with an H in their names into the fire or gas chamber. Helena, you too, you too......" (Helena keeps talking to herself.)

Sasha: This is something we cannot mention! And no longer need to mention! Everyone knows that is an overblown lie.

Pina: You're the one who's lying.

Sasha: Then what should we do? Spit at all of the aboveground society, roar at them? It's been more than a year, this is all coming to an end, but you still want to force all of the aboveground into despair all to show the great pain you have suffered!

Pina: There has never been an end.

Sasha: (suddenly soft) I don't know who you wish to torture. (Looking at Helena)

Pina: I just don't want myself to seem accepting of an illusion of peace.

Sasha: But you are.

Pina: We all are.

Sasha: What a joke! Pina, don't force everyone to look at the enormous wound of the underground people! To no avail! I will keep marching forward, ever since watching my mother drop dead at the concentration camp; here in the aboveground society, I need to play according to their rules to survive. (go to Helena's side) You don't need memories. If there are memories of the underground, then there will be images of her brother being stampeded to a pulp by the aboveground people right in front her as they were escaping, or images of father thrown into the pond to rot away. Helena, look how beautiful your clothes are, look, you haven't been sent to the gas chamber or the incinerator. The gentlemen were joking with you, were they not?

Helena: Yes.

Sasha: Pina, we are fortunate to have left the damp underground, even if the sun is too hot or too scorching that it makes us swell with pain in just 10 minutes. Helena...... look how bright this room is, how dry.

Helena: But my skin is so dry that it's cracking.

Sasha: Look how beautiful the sunset is outside.

Helena: But we swell and itch with pain if we're in the sun for too long.

Sasha: And there's running water just by opening the tap.

Helena: But tap water has a pungent chemical smell.

Sasha: (furious) This is the life that you must live! Stop complaining like a child! Your brother tried to escape and was stamped into a pulp, have you forgotten? Your mother died next to you with a metal stick shoved in her lower body, have you also forgotten? Stop being so unreasonable! Helena, stop thinking you are a pure girl anymore, accept the life you have now and live it!

(Helena storms off, picks up a doll that has a metal stick shoved in its lower body.)

Helena: Mother, dear Mother, why are you not moving? Just yesterday you kept telling me not to open my eyes, not to look, to fall fast asleep, sleep! Today it's you who won't open your eyes. Mother, touch my face look at me. I won't cry, and I won't ask anymore why everyone saw brother get stomped to death and couldn't help......

Sasha: Helena !

Helena: (goes towards Sasha) Mother, dear mother, how did you die from one shove of a metal pipe? Before, I was shoved so many times by so many gentlemen! They kept saying it was so dirty, but kept shoving it in me. Mother, I'm still alive, why are you dead?

Sasha: Stop your daydreaming.

Helena: Yes, dear sister; I want to accept the life I have now and live it.

Pina: Helena.

Sasha: Very good.

Helena: So, what should I do now?

Sasha: Perhaps you can read some books; perhaps you could ask Pina, maybe she knows some things from Mr. Adolf that she hasn't told us.

Helena: Dear sister Pina, what has Mr. Adolf told you?

Pina: Nothing, really.

Sasha: So, some people take it seriously and don't even tell their "own people".

Helena: I beg of you to tell us, so many days now and no one has come to see us, please! Please tell Mr. Adolf that I'm bored into a panic and spending my days daydreaming! I've been dreaming all day that they pushed my little brother with a bam, and he fell to the floor. Mother didn't even look once. Or tell Mr. Adolf to give us work...... other than reading.

Pina: Dear Helena, Adolf did not tell me anything and has absolutely no work to give us; I asked him last time, do you remember?

Helena: Adolf, Adolf, he's MR. Adolf, not just Adolf. But......
Mr. Adolf won't give us any work? Is it really like what that gentleman was saying?

Sasha: Helena! What did you just say?

Pina: Oh, Helena.

Sasha: What did that gentleman say?

Helena: The gentleman from last time said, Mr. Adolf will force us back down to the underground.

Sasha: My goodness, this is not true! (pause) Pina, do you know anything about this?

Pina: I'm not quite sure.

Sasha: Helena, why did that gentleman say that?

Helena: That gentleman said people aboveground are starting to discover how the government has been using violence and slaughter upon underground people. Incinerators have been spitting out odorous black smoke around the clock. One incinerator burns out, two more are built, two burn out then four new ones are built......

Pina: The gentleman also said, "So, now take advantage of this beneficial lean toward underground people, you must be very happy about this! Dirty underground people can also be taken seriously, the underground people can work aboveground; but the aboveground definitely does not have so much work for you all; get ready to roll back to your rat nests."

Helena: But first let me get off again......

Sasha: Helena, why did you not tell me?

Helena: I was afraid it was true, if I said it.

Sasha: But you told Pina?

Pina: I thought she had been acting weird lately, so I forced it out of Helena.

Sasha: Helena! I think I've told you before, I should be the first person you tell if anything happens! I am the leader here, have you forgotten?

Helena: I'm sorry.

Sasha: So, Mr. Adolf also told you the same thing?

Pina: Mr. Adolf...... he didn't say clearly, but he hinted a little.

Sasha: None of you even told me.

Helena: (crying) Sasha, I'm sorry! I was too scared. I really want to go back! But my father, mother, older brother, baby brother can no longer go back with me. There is only me, alone. The thought of that makes me so scared, so scared.

Sasha: Helena, don't cry anymore; (limp) then what should we do? I don't want to go back to the dark and damp underground.

Helena: My father won't be there to help me chase away a wall of cockroaches.

Sasha: How can he? How can Mr. Adolf allow something like this to happen? We are his top underground models.

Pina: This is all just a rumor. There's no need to believe that it's true.

Sasha: Pina, is that so? We aren't like you. We don't have Mr. Adolf to back us up like you do.

Helena: We're not like Pina?

Sasha: That's right; Helena, we have not gained Mr. Adolf's favor, so we will be sent back; but Pina...... won't.

Pina: No, of course not. Helena, don't listen to Sasha's nonsense.

Helena: Then I'll be sent back to a home with only me living in it. I don't want that! How terrible! How terrible! Dear sister Pina, Dear sister Pina, can you help us tell Mr. Adolf not to send us back? Please.

Pina: This is only a rumor. Plus, I would be sent back with you, as well.

Helena: I don't want that! I don't want that!

Sasha: Mr. Adolf no longer needs model underground people. We are no use anymore? Weren't we supposed to succeed and use our success to transform into aboveground people? Weren't we supposed to show all the aboveground people that underground people could also be well-groomed and virtuous? How can Mr. Adolf do this to us?

Helena: (murmuring) Guns...... then we can only resort to using guns.

Pina: No! Helena.

Sasha: Guns? Helena what guns are you talking about?

Pina: Helena, you can't...... I beg you.

Helena: That gentleman gave me a gun.

Pina: No.

Sasha: Why?

Helena: He said we can use the gun to force Mr. Adolf to let us
stay.

Sasha: Why did the gentleman tell you this?

Pina: Sasha, Helena; give up this stupid idea, please.

Helena: That gentleman said all the bad things that have
happened to underground people were instructed by Mr.
Adolf, Mr. Adolf is the top decision maker. If we wish to
stay, we must use the gun to force Mr. Adolf, or even......

Sasha:...... or even?

Pina: Or even kill him as revenge for underground people; but
this is not real. This is just a feud among aboveground
people! We do not have to let underground people become

scapegoats.

Sasha: But us being sent back underground is an indisputable fact.

Pina: Everything is still uncertain...... !

Sasha: Pina! For once, only for once, please stand together with us.

Pina: I've always been standing together with you all.

Sasha: Helena, you don't want to go back to the underground either, right? (Helena nods) Then let us pick up that gun, and go find Mr. Adolf.

(Lights out)

(Lights brighten slowly, Adolf paces back and forth on stage, Prime Minister enters with the gentlemen)

Prime Minister: Adolf.

(Everyone echoes)

Adolf: Mr. Prime Minister and gentlemen, good evening.

Prime Minister: Congratulations on your exemplary service.

Adolf: Thank you.

A: Adolf is a youth to be regarded with respect.

B: Isn't he? Not only for developing the underworld......

C: He was even able to find the cure for AIDS from the underground world.

A: When on a lucky streak, good performance comes even when lying down.

B: Adolf performance comes from lying down?

(B grabs Adolf's butt, everyone laughs.)

Adolf: May I ask to what do we owe this special visit, Mr. Prime Minister? New work orders?

C: Such a smart lad.

A: Yes, yes, as they say, "one never goes to the temple for

nothing."

Prime Minister: Okay, stop teasing the boy, he is my top successor.

B: Whoa! Whoa! Whoa! Everyone look here, the cabinet Prime Minister has been hand-picked.

A: Then we should be a little more polite.

C: So, that little lady named Agneta has no hope now?

B: Oh well ~ yes!

C: Doesn't this mean Prime Minister is picking on her?

(everyone laughs)

Prime Minister: Enough, enough, dear Adolf, in addition to the development of underground society with the AIDS antidote and vaccine R&D, how is the development of new energy?

Adolf: Mr. Prime Minister, unfortunately, we have discovered that other than small amounts of bio gas found in a few specific locations, there are no possible signs of oil or precious metals as estimated during the initial exploration.

Prime Minister: Is that so?

A: Mr. Prime Minister, that's enough. Otherwise underground

development will send Adolf's momentum soaring, and he will be riding over your head.

Adolf: Nothing of the sorts, I have achieved what I have because I worked in accordance with instructions of the Prime Minister.

C: You really know how to talk.

B: Haha, this lad really has a future.

Prime Minister: Mhmm.

Adolf: Mr. Prime Minister, I will have the underground energy exploration progress report on your desk tomorrow.

Prime Minister: No need, it's almost time to pull out.

Adolf: What you mean is to stop the energy development and......

B: What?

C: And?

A, B, C: And then?

Prime Minister: Adolf, what do you say?

Adolf: Evacuate the underground, destroy both concentration camps and gas chambers. Destroy information that may cause any public debate.

Prime Minister: Smart.

A, B, C: Very smart!

Adolf: I will have a few trusted aides carry this out. I estimate completion within three days.

Prime Minister: Mhmm, then what about the underground people in the concentration camps?

(pause)

Adolf: Reporting to Prime Minister, we will set up temporary shelter for the underground people to be resettled, and will counsel them into……

A, B, C: Hee hee hee.

A: Like I said, he's still young.

C: Really naive.

Prime Minister: Adolf, can you create a file of all the underground people in concentration camps within three days?

Adolf: Currently there are hundreds of camps around the country, to complete within three days would indeed be difficult.

Prime Minister: What if there is no need to create a file?

(A, B, C laugh.)

Adolf: Mr. Prime Minister, I don't really understand what you mean.

C: Like I said, he's still new at this.

B: Hee hee hee, how could he not understand this little piece of logic?

Prime Minister: If they don't exist, why would they need to have files created?

Adolf: Reporting to Prime Minister, hundreds of concentration camps hold about 1.3 million people......

C: In fact, concentration camps don't have any underground people.

B: There is no one at all.

A: It was just a temporary residence for the underground for the early stage of mining.

B: Half way through, we began gradually guiding underground people back to the underground.

(A, B, C chuckling)

Prime Minister: Adolf, I expect great things from you! You will not let me down. Adolf: Yes, concentration camps had no underground people staying there from mid-term on, so I will send people to "clean up."

Prime Minister: Clean up? (laughs) Yes, yes. Adolf, make sure you clean it well, if you don't, it will be dusty. That wouldn't be too good, would it?

Adolf: Yes.

Prime Minister: Adolf, where will you dispose of the trash?

Adolf: When developing underground energy, there was a deep 1.2 km hole that was dug north of the border.

Prime Minister: Mhmm. Do it well, when you finish, come have a meal with us.

Adolf: Yes.

(Prime Minister and others turned to leave.)

Prime Minister: Oh, yes, Adolf; be sure to dispose of the three protocols.

Adolf: But with their popularity in the aboveground......

Prime Minister: I heard that they want to take the fine education and order of the aboveground back to the underground.

A: You heard about such a thing?

B, C: Yes.

A: From who?

B: Mr. Prime Minister.

(A, B, C laugh)

Adolf: Mr. Prime Minister, the underground world may now already be too inconvenient to live in, since they have received good training and education, can it be?

Prime Minister: To nurture a tiger brings calamity; this is how it will be settled; as for not being able to live after returning to the underground, that's their problem.

Adolf: I understand.

Prime Minister: Let's go.

B: Hee, hee, hee.

A: What a shame, no toys anymore.

B: Where else do you think we're going?

A, B, C: To pick toys. (turns head) Adolf, do the job well.

Adolf: Good night, everyone.

(Prime Minister and A, B, C walk pass Adolf and leave, immediately taking off clothes in a pile, and place doll heads on top that become Sasha, Helena and Pina; the three are slightly nervous but try to stay calm.)

Sasha, Helena, Pina: Mr. Adolf, hello, long time no see.

(The three, in order, welcomed Adolf with kisses on his left and right cheeks.)

Sasha: May I ask what brings Mr. Adolf to see us today?

Adolf: Go back.

(everyone stunned)

Sasha: Go back? We just got here?

Adolf: I said go back.

Sasha: Mr. Adolf, you are joking with us? We were just learning about environmental sanitation ......

Adolf: You don't understand what I mean?

Helena: But Mr. Adolf, you have really confused us...... (Adolf looks coldly at the three of them, they begin to panic)

Sasha: Mr. Adolf, please do not make this kind of joke.

Helena: We have been working on new media recently, Mr. Adolf, it will be on display next Tuesday.

Sasha: Yes, and we intend on inviting you, Mr. Adolf, as the special guest for the ribbon cutting at the opening ceremony.

Adolf: No need, just go back.

Sasha: Mr. Adolf, we really don't know where you want us to go back to?

Helena: So, would you be willing to be our special guest for the ribbon cutting at the opening ceremony?

Adolf: No need to waste your energy.

Sasha: Where can we go if we have to leave?

(long pause)

Pina: Please, Mr. Adolf, tell us your decision directly, do not tease us.

(long pause)

Adolf: Underground.

(long pause)

Sasha: No! Mr. Adolf, you cannot do this to us. Now you want us to return to the dirty, damp underground, then what?

Helena: We can not live all day in dark place anymore.

Sasha: Dirty water constantly oozes from the pores of the rock walls, mice brush by at any time. And cockroaches! There are cockroaches with a variety of disgusting, infectious bacteria, that climb over your mouth in your sleep, trying to get into your ears and nose.

Helena: I have trouble breathing just thinking about it.

Sasha: If we don't have clean tap water, how are we going to clean ourselves?

Helena: How can contaminated water be drinkable?

Sasha: Dear Mr. Adolf, please don't treat us this way.

Helena: What can we do?

Adolf: That's your problem.

Pina: Mr. Adolf, is there really no other choices?

(Adolf looks at Pina.)

Adolf: Unfortunately, this is the final decision.

Pina: When do we have to leave?

Adolf: Seven days from now, a professional will send you back.

(Sasha looks at the two of them, puts hand in her own

little tote.)

Pina: How can you do this to us?

Adolf: Rats can only be with rats...

Pina: Wolves can only be with wolves, foxes can only be with foxes, geese can only mate with other geese, as to maintain the purity of the species.

Adolf: Absolutely no cat will fall in love with a rat, the people aboveground have the same obligation.

Sasha: Mr. Adolf, we know that you are an influential big shot; (pause) please make your final reconsideration.

(Adolf looked puzzled at Sasha.)

Sasha: (slightly threatening) Please seriously consider our request.

Pina: (nervously) Mr. Adolf, this is our last request.

Adolf: (laughs) Regrettably ...

(Sasha takes out the gun)

Sasha: You shouldn't have treated us this way!

(Helena begins to cry.)

Sasha: Now, please solemnly reconsider, and let us stay

aboveground.

Adolf: (to Pina) Did you know about this action?

Sasha: Adolf! Look at me!

Pina: I knew.

Adolf: You agreed?

Pina: Yes, I participated.

Sasha: Shut up! Now the gun is in my hands, you have no right to ask questions. Promise us, let us stay. (Adolf looks coldly at Sasha; long pause) Enough! Don't cry!

(Helena lowers down her crying.)

Helena: It is really horrifying to do this.

Sasha: You agreed then.

Helena: I know.

Sasha: Then you shouldn't feel regret.

Adolf: (To Pina) You really disappoint me.

Pina: We had no choice.

Sasha: Now go make the phone calls, let us stay.

Adolf: Who provided you with the gun?

Helena: It was the bald gentleman.

Sasha: Stop talking.

Adolf: So you think the gun can change your future?

Pina: This is our last, and only way.

Sasha: It's not your turn to question us, if you wish to walk out alive……

Adolf: Then I shall make the call?

Sasha: Correct!

Adolf: Who should I call?

Sasha: Don't ask us! Ask yourself!

Helena: If you want to live, Mr. Adolf.

Sasha: Helena! Shut up!

Helena: Why do you want me to shut up? (getting close to Sasha) Shut up! Shut up! Am I not one of those who will be sent back to the underground world?

Sasha: Don't say such things at this moment! Out of my way!

Helena: Dear sister Sasha, do you think you can control everything or command us just by having a gun in your hands? (Reaches out to grab the gun)

Sasha: What are you doing? Stop!

Helena: This gun was given to me by that gentleman! I should hold it. Why are you always the one to take control!

Sasha: Let go! Where is that gentleman of yours? You have so many gentlemen, do you really remember who he is? Is he the one who like to do doggy-style from the back? Or the one who electroshocked your vagina? Let go!

Helena: Give me the gun! It's all your fault! My first night I had no idea how many gentlemen did me, one after another! Until I had absolutely no feeling, semen kept flowing from my vagina, and they still kept doing me.

Sasha: You can't blame that on me!

Helena: Only if you didn't sell me out.

Sasha: Then I would be raped instead!

Helena: They casted water into my mouth, my body, and then beat me up, and make me throw out the water. The water flows out, as if to wash my filthy underground body. And then they did it again, and again, and again ……

Sasha: Stop your self-pity. We are all the same in the end.

Helena: But you make everyone your subordinates! No one

understands you, you are the rare one. You made yourself Queen!

Pina: Helena......

Sasha: Shut up! Helena, stop talking in your own logic.

Helena: In my logic! So, I'm blocking you now, preventing you from becoming a hero of reform, am I?

Sasha: Let go!

Helena: I have more to say! Because you can not have Adolf, so you point a gun at him.

Sasha: Shut up.

Helena: You're jealous about Pina. She has won more trust from Adolf.

Sasha: Shut up.

Helena: So you could only continuously rat us out! Play petty games! You wanted to get rid of Pina! But you have failed.

Sasha: Shut up.

Helena: Go be your underground queen! Cockroaches and rats will be thrilled to kiss your toes.

Sasha: Shut up.

Helena: Then you can only look up to Adolf and Pina, who have so much love for each other.

Sasha: Enough! (Sasha pushes Helena hard to the ground and looks at Adolf) Are you happy to see us fighting amongst ourselves? This is what you wanted, right?

Adolf: I did not ask you to put on an for me.

Sasha: What?

Adolf: And a bad act, for that matter.

Sasha: Don't think I'm afraid to shoot!

Pina: Sasha! Don't forget why we are here.

Sasha: I know, of course I know. We want the right to live aboveground permanently.

Adolf: What do you have for bargaining?

Sasha: Your life!

Adolf: My life.

Helena: This chip isn't valuable enough? Then our revolutionary heroic uprising will fail.

Pina: Helena.

Sasha: I'm going to count to three, if you don't answer I'm

doing to shoot.

Adolf: Sasha, so what if you shoot? What can change by killing me? So that you can stay aboveground? In prison?

Pina: Mr. Adolf.

Sasha: Mr. Adolf? Pfff! Adolf, you best not be thinking about stalling with word games. One!

Adolf: Then just shoot, why count? Because when you were dug up aboveground from the underground like rats, that's when you should have taken this shot, but you didn't! All the brave and rebellious of the underground people were all taken to concentration camps or gas chambers. When they worked for more than 20 hours a day for a piece of bread and a bowl of soup, where were you? The vast majority of the pitiful underground people still think they will live well. Concentration camp is nothing but a terrifying rumor. It's not until they are really sent there that they begin to complain about the world being unfair, that there's no God. Even if God growled in your ears, you still feel the need to guard your small mouse nest, so as to protect your only property!

Pina: Mr. Adolf, please stop!

Sasha: Two.

Adolf: Your miserable pack of worthless rats only know how to blink your tiny little eyes while you lick your tiny little wounds, calculating your own meager efforts; and still who do you wish to come and give you hope? But do not knowing that the leader who tried to lead you out of the voice died early in your own indifference. Underground people can only be reduced to domestic helpers, sex toys and fertilizers; while lamenting their own fates, and only able to lament their own fates; for compatriots will only frame each other, they do not care about each other, and will fight against each other; no matter from underground to aboveground, from happiness to despair, you never truly know what is unity. Why haven't you opened fired? If your killing me can change the whole system, then do it! I don't mind at all, because Adolfs will continue to appear by your side one after another, controlling left and right your life decisions, dominating you until you die under your own indifference. (long pause) Three!

(Sasha is shocked, pulls the trigger but it couldn't be fired; Adolf takes the gun and loads it.)

Pina: (to Adolf) What can we do now?

Adolf: Just accept it. (Pulls trigger, gun fires. Adolf exits. Other than the women sobbing, there was only silence, for a long time.)

Helena: I've told you. I should have held the gun.

Sasha: You should show me how to use it.

Helena: Dear sister Sasha, I know you admire Mr. Adolf, so how could I teach you how to use the gun? If you fired the gun because of personal feelings, what should sister Pina and I do?

Sasha: You've changed, Helena.

Helena: This might be something you taught me.

Sasha: What else can we do? Go back to the underground? No way!

(Sasha and Helena start sobbing)

Sasha: (suddenly thinks of something) Protest? Yes! Use an elegant solution! We should go to the streets to protest, letting everyone know that underground people should be taken seriously, too.

(Lights dim)

(metronome clicks in rhythm as lights brighten, the three women execute each day of protest in accordance to the rhythm of the metronome; get up, wash, go out; parading for appeals, they kept saying the following.)

Sasha: Underground people also have good virtue.

Helena: Please value underground human rights.

Pina: We should not be sacrificed.

Sasha: Please stand up and support the underground people.

Helena: Underground people and aboveground people equally enjoy the sun.

Sasha: Sasha: Please protect us, allowing the aboveground world to not only have one kind of view.

(gather for speeches)

Sasha: Underground people are educated as aboveground people. They learn aboveground law and lifestyle. Now the underground people have learned successfully and have shown our characteristics, we are asked to return underground. This is no doubt wiping out the basic rights of underground people, ignoring the wishes of underground people! For underground people, this is undoubtedly a tyrannical policy. We plea to all virtuous, outstanding aboveground people to come together. Stand up and support underground people!

Helena, Pina: Please support the underground people.

Sasha, Helena, Pina: Please support the underground people!

(crowd disperses, each doing their own things, sleep. Keep repeating aforementioned actions. Repeat process four times, gradually lowering voice, with the fourth only contains action and mouth movement. Lights slowly fade, while lights are on in another section, where Adolf and Agneta coldly watch.)

Agneta: Protests have started.

Adolf: So?

Agneta: You're not worried?

Adolf: What is there to worry about?

Agneta: If they succeed, they will be able to stay aboveground.

Adolf: Mhmm.

Agneta: Then they will have more time to open their big mouths and expose information to the blood-thirsty media.

Adolf: Mhmm.

Agneta: And your political career will be over.

Adolf: Mhmm.

(long pause, Agneta profoundly looks at Adolf)

Agneta: Adolf, I don't know when you become so generous.

Adolf: What do you mean?

Agneta: For example...... six days until repatriation. (pause) Anyone with a brain knows how dramatic will the next seven days be. Half a year ago, we all thought that the underground people were beasts, uncivilized apes, the government was able to arbitrarily...... "use" them. But now we all know that they are just a nation that hid underground after a war, so "using" them has become not as convenient as before, even troublesome. But there are always a group of self-righteous and pro-democratic activists in the media who like to disclose government's previous tyrannies.

(long pause)

Agneta: Although you and I seem like rivals, I should remind you not to let things get too complicated. People above us will be very unhappy, Adolf.

Adolf: You are so talkative today.

Agneta: (slightly resentful) I know what happened yesterday.

Adolf: What?

Agneta: The three women barged into the office with a gun threatening you to keep them permanently aboveground. (pause) You couldn't make a decision and for the sake of saving your own life, you offered them the condition of seven days to fight for the opportunity to stay, hoping to use the masses and the power of the media to force authorities to concur.

Adolf: Agneta, you have quite an imagination.

Agneta: Adolf! You can remain calm and composed while watching this farce all you want, but you should know this ball of fire will soon or later burn you. How will the media report it then? The most favored cabinet prime minister successor illegally persecuted underground people.

Adolf: What about you?

Agneta: (stunned) What?

Adolf: Being the head of education, but using inhumane and
corporal punishment to educate the underground people.
Would someone who might be the first female cabinet prime
minister do such things?

Agneta: Childish! I received orders to deal with them in a very
harsh way, so they could not engage in riots. They needed
discipline, did you know? Those bitches had to learn their
place, and more importantly, understand why they were
here. There was only one way to make them understand:
discipline, harsh discipline. If you want to keep control of
them, this is the secret.

Adolf: Is that so?

Agneta: In my opinion, it is right for the government to do so, to
me it's right as well. I have no authority to do any personal
thinking or to have any personal thoughts or feelings. On
the contrary, my duty is to comply with top-level orders
without objection, even if those orders mean to kill millions

of people with poisonous gas, I am also willing to implement. Believe me, that is why I can not allow myself to have the slightest sympathy for those women.

(long pause, the two watch the three women's silent protest)

Agneta: (dryly) I am always devoted and committed to fulfilling my duty, and I've always been proud of belonging to the noble aboveground society, I feel valued.

Adolf: I'm sorry to hear you say that.

(Agneta has a stunned expression)

Adolf: Agneta, I've always thought of you as a worthy opponent.

Agneta: Don't think giving them seven days makes you more merciful! We are all on the same boat! When trouble breaks out, no one will be better off. How many dirty deeds have you done? You carry millions of lives on your conscience!

Adolf: Adolf: I am, I indeed carried out each task, but I've never stopped cursing myself. (long pause) No one can stay. Everyone is tired of this play. It's time to put on a new show.

(silence, the two watch the three women's silent protest)

Agneta: Adolf, pray to God this farce can come to an end.

(Agneta walks away. The lights dim, while the lights are dimming Sasha tears open her shirt and exposes her breasts.)

Sasha: I beg you all to look at us! We are underground people who are rich in etiquette! Please protect us! Please listen to our voice.

(lights darken in disgust)

(light on, Adolf and Agneta each in their lit sections, loud noisy music.)

Agneta: (frightened) As an educator, I am proud of my work, but this is also the glory of the aboveground society! Please applaud what I do!

(Agneta stumbles down the bench. Adolf opens a lollipop and takes a few mouthfuls before putting it aside; raises his pistol to his temple and opens fire, light dims, gunshot echoes endlessly until the underground cave area lights up.

The three women mournfully look at the underground cave.)

Pina: We're …… home.

Helena: How did this happen? How did this happen?

Pina: Aside from us, how many others are still alive?

Helena: I have no father, no mother, no older brother, no baby brother, only I'm left, only I'm left.

Pina: You still have us, three of us.

Sasha: Mr. Adolf, Mr. Adolf really treated us this way, then sadly killed himself.

Helena: He killed himself, to let us live, what is the use?

(pause)

Pina: Starry Night, Van gogh's Starry Night, sparkle after sparkle, and the sounds and smells of the underground.

Sasha: No more.

Pina: (firmly) Not anymore.

Helena: Not anymore.

Pina: Today we shall talk about art.

(Three laugh, slightly whispering.)

Helena: I am sure that all of you are very surprised that we would return underground and accept the changes in cultural society.

Pina: Like re-discovering the truth in a dark corridor.

Sasha: Is this what they called "enlightenment"?

Pina: (Extremely gently) Quite right, I believe. At last......

Sasha: we still return to the womb of Mother Earth.

(Light slowly shines through the depths of the cave, Sasha firmly walks into the depths of the cave, Pina hesitates for a while, but takes Helena's hand and follows in. Captions read, "It is said that when the three women returned into the depths of the cave, they found the legendary pure land. There was light, green pastures and flowers, and precious stones and resources. From then on, no one has ever seen them again.")

The End

穢土天堂：穢土天堂首部曲

作　　者／鍾伯淵
社　　長／林宜澐
總 編 輯／廖志墭
英文翻譯／倪湘鈴
英文編校／游文綺
中文校對／江子逸
編輯協力／葉育伶、林韋聿
書籍設計／三人制創
內文排版／藍天圖物宣字社

出　　版／蔚藍文化出版股份有限公司
　　　　　地址：10667臺北市大安區復興南路二段237號13樓
　　　　　電話：02-7710-7864　傳真：02-7710-7868
　　　　　臉書：https://www.facebook.com/AZUREPUBLISH/
　　　　　讀者服務信箱：azurebks@gmail.com

總 策 畫／曉劇場 Shinehouse Theatre
　　　　　地址：台北市萬華區環河南路二段125巷15弄21號
　　　　　電話：0953-186-507
　　　　　觀眾服務信箱：Shinehouse0820@gmail.com

總 經 銷／大和書報圖書股份有限公司
　　　　　地址：24890新北市新莊市五工五路2號
　　　　　電話：02-8990-2588

法律顧問／眾律國際法律事務所　著作權律師／范國華律師
　　　　　電話：02-2759-5585　網站：www.zoomlaw.net

印　　刷／世和印製企業有限公司
定　　價／台幣280元

初版一刷／2017年11月
ISBN 978-986-94403-5-6

※本書獲文化部贊助出版

MINISTRY OF CULTURE

國家圖書館出版品預行編目（CIP）資料

穢土天堂：穢土天堂首部曲 / 鍾伯淵著.
-- 初版. -- 臺北市：蔚藍文化, 2017.11
　　面；　公分
ISBN 978-986-94403-5-6（平裝）

854.6　　　　　　　　　　106018716

在阿道夫舉槍自盡前的
自白:「我確實的執行
任務,但我從來沒有在
心裡停止詛咒自己。」
(2011 / 攝影-王捷)

為了不被送回被掏空的地下世界，三名女子走上街頭爭取權益：「請站出來聲援地底人，地上人、地底人平等享受陽光。」（2011 / 攝影-王捷）

求你們看看我們吧！我們是富有禮教的地底人，請聽聽我們的聲音。（2011 / 攝影-王捷）

阿道夫背負著開發地下世界最高領導者的名號與長官們的期許，無情的帶領軍隊屠殺地下世界人。
（2011 / 攝影-王捷）

上　在開發地底人的熱潮過去後，總理大人指示阿道夫「清掃」集中營上百萬的地底人，並
　　將所有「垃圾」掩埋至北方的地洞中。（2011 / 攝影-王捷）

下　抽菸的女子。（2011 / 攝影-王捷）

狹小的淋浴間宛若傳聞中的毒氣室，三名女子害怕的放聲尖叫。（2011 / 攝影-王捷）

教好這些母豬，接下來我要看她們不斷出
現在電視上，裝出一副溫柔賢淑的樣子，
好去堵住反對開發地底社會的聲浪。
（2011 / 攝影-王捷）

親愛的媽媽，妳為什麼一動也不動？昨天妳還一直叫我不要睜開眼睛、
不要看、快睡、快睡！今天換妳不睜開眼睛；媽媽，摸摸我的臉看看我
（2011／攝影-王捷）

「我們是行禮如儀的女子，禮儀懸掛在我們眼前。」三名女子被迫學習禮儀、美學和藝術，以向社會大眾展示地底人受到良好的待遇。（2011／攝影-王捷）

海倫娜：我會努力記得。什麼是請？請是拜託，所以要拜求他們放過我的時候，我要說請放過我、請放過我、請放過我。（2011／攝影-王捷）

教育首長艾妮塔在總理大人的指示下，
以野獸的方式指導地下女子們如何成為
優雅的地上人。（2011 / 攝影-王捷）

《穢土天堂》二〇一一年曉劇場演出宣傳海報

穢土天堂首部曲

穢土天堂

Armageddon

鍾伯淵 著

目錄
CONTENTS

推薦序 《穢土天堂》的當代警世寓言

文／于善祿（臺北藝術大學戲劇學系助理教授）

《穢土天堂》，從劇名來看，就充滿了強烈的矛盾感，既是天堂，卻非樂土或淨土，而是穢土，那究竟是一個怎麼樣的所在？這個所在是如何形成的？而那裡的人又是如何自處？這個劇本的場景構成及流轉，具有高度的影視鏡頭感，人物形象及性格亦鮮明立判，對於人性的刻劃更是鞭辟入裡，即使先前已經觀賞過戲劇的演出，印象畫面仍然深刻，再有機會細讀劇本，仍覺劇力萬鈞，力透紙背，而劇中所涉及的現實、極端與殘酷，既令人愁眉不舒，也教人脊樑發冷，低迴再三！

從空間場景來看，劇本以教育展示開啟，以抗議訴願而逐漸落幕，主

要的行動者都是劇中的三名女角：莎夏、海倫娜、碧娜；不過前者乃是作為地上社會教育部對地底人施行禮儀教育的成果展現，隱含著創作者對於制式僵化教育模式的諷刺及批判；後者則是為了爭取不想重返地下社會所作的抗爭遊行，最終仍只是一場早知結局的失敗革命。在場面調度上，都運用了重複、累積、加強意象的手法，而不論是被動的展示，或是主動的爭取，最後都完全無法改變那巨大的階級科層與權力結構。

很明顯地，在這個「穢土天堂」裡，有地上與地下兩個社會空間。地上社會代表的是文化陶冶、社交禮儀、藝術素養、優雅品格等，而這一切都必須透過教育才能逐漸養成，然而極其諷刺地，我們在劇中所看到的是，所謂的「教育專家」艾妮塔，服從上級長官的命令，忠誠地執行教育地底人的任務，以鞭打（打屁股）及斥罵的方式，灌輸三位女主角以相關的知識模式與言行規範，將其視為教育展示的「樣品」。地下社會則代表野蠻、未開化、具攻擊性、藝術、美、教育，均付之厥如，第二部曲《地

下女子》將有更多篇幅的描繪。

而不論是地上或地下社會，均由總理大人及內閣大臣們治理管控。除了教育部門的鞭打斥罵教育之外，還有地下開發部對於地底沼氣的開發計畫，這個計畫還附帶「清掃」地底人的種族滅絕政策；除此之外，更有總理大人與「先生們」恣意地享受地底人的性服務，將其視為隨取隨用、即丟即棄的「性玩具」。地上社會與地下社會之間，完全不可能翻轉。

在一場介於阿道夫與碧娜的對話中，可以清楚地看到不同社會的兩人，對於「使用展示地底人漂白整個地下世界開發計畫」的（假）慈悲與仇恨、救恩與原諒之間的辯論，看似正義殿堂的（偽）展示，事實上這是一場權力不對等的對話，也是一場關於「忠實的執行」與「平庸的邪惡」的對話，兩人都處在極端變形扭曲的人性空間與極權結構之中，無法翻身、不可置換、沒有原諒的恆惡與永恨之間。

除了不同社會階層之間的強烈矛盾，即使同在一個社界，也處處充滿

衝突與競爭，爾虞我詐，人不為己，天誅地滅。譬如阿道夫與艾妮塔，兩位部長級的官員，對於地底人的挑選、教育、訓練、溝通的方式，通通不同，兩人也經常為此而彼此冷眼旁觀或是幸災樂禍；而「先生們」對於阿道夫的地底人處置與地底開發計畫，在總理大人及阿道夫面前，同樣是逢迎拍馬或冷嘲熱諷，呈現一幅地上人也有地上人苦惱的景象。

地底人三名女角之間，莎夏為了想成為地上人而認同艾妮塔的教育方式，且巴結阿道夫，甚至還提供出海倫娜是處女，促使她必須「服務」總理大人及許多「先生們」；碧娜則認清現實，她及她的家人雖然救了摔進地洞的阿道夫，但她卻認為這完全改變不了什麼。三人對於刺殺阿道夫的計畫，立場與看法不同，莎夏還認為海倫娜、碧娜都分與地上人之間有秘密協議，致使三人之間的互信基礎崩解，產生內鬨，而所謂的依賴，也都只是利用。

這齣戲的確會讓人聯想到納粹 國、迫害猶太人、集中營、毒氣室

等，或許有人會問，這和當代台灣社會有什麼關係？所有的歷史其實都是當代（史），以史為鑑，見往知來，更何況在所有的人類文明發展過程當中，人性的發展是最緩慢的。在價值系統混亂、正義亂轉型、民主不法治、權力即傲慢的年代，細讀這個劇本，仍有其強烈而深沉的當代警世意義。

推薦序 《穢土天堂》裡的質疑

文／梁紅玉（資深媒體人）

劇場擔負了怎樣的社會責任？劇作家又基於怎樣的理念從事創作？被喻為「波蘭劇場界蕭邦」的猶太裔導演瓦里科夫斯基曾經表示：「若這個世界真的美好，到超市購物就可以了，不用花時間進劇場看戲」，簡明扼要地回答了我們的提問。至於「曉劇場」編導鍾伯淵，則在一趟德國旅遊參訪後有感而發，以納粹的荒謬行徑為本，寫下了《穢土天堂》首部曲，進而質疑社會建構中的種種神話。

神話是什麼？神話可以是故事；也可能指某種意識型態，其目的在於提供我們一種理解世界的方式，但別以為神話就只是好聽的故事，社會學理論也指出：「一個成功的神話，必須把支配團體的利益加以自然化和普

遍化」。於是，整齣戲就藉由看似輕巧愉悅的對話，堆疊出沉重且沉痛的悲鳴。

莎：我相信在座各位必定對我們重回地上，接受文化社會陶冶的改變感到十分驚奇。

海：如同在黑暗的甬道重新尋獲真理。

莎：這就叫重見天日嗎？

海、碧：可不是嘛。

海：一開始我們並不瞭解禮儀。

碧：美學。

莎：和社會規範。

好一段冠冕堂皇的台詞，不是？三名地下社會的女子，有幸被挑選至

地上社會接受教育、進行所謂的文化洗禮，除了學習「禮儀、美學和社會規範」外，還負責展示改造成果，並進一步為地上高層提供性服務。以至於在文本中，當這些愉悅而輕巧的對話，一而再地被重覆再重覆，最終淪為機械式的空洞聲音後，就不禁想起傅柯（Michel Foucault）論述的權力關係與「規訓」一詞，傅柯認為「統治並非只是思想上的控制」，當權者會透過「某種姿態、某些話語、某些慾望」的強制力去馴化被統治者的身體，久而久之，受支配者將不假思索地去行動實踐。以此類推，宗教戒律、學校教育乃至於軍事化訓練，不都以一種枝微末結的規範去要求我們，從而完成支配與管理？那，文化的侵略呢？《黑皮膚白面具》書中，被法國殖民的阿爾及利亞人，甚至以會說流利的法語自豪。

碧：相信諸位必定想問「地下」是否有藝術、有美、有教育。

莎：十分遺憾的是，沒有。因此我們萬分感謝，阿道夫先生。

海：以及令我們得以重拾生命真諦的艾妮塔女士。

相較於那些受教化的地下人，或出於無奈或基於自保，而出現某種令人難以理解的行徑；負責教育地下人的地上階級，面對女人們被輪暴，甚而施暴、送入毒氣室，又怎樣去合理化自己的作為？

艾：我總是虔誠而投入地執行任務，也始終為自己屬於地上社會的高貴人種而感到驕傲，感到有價值……。

莎：海倫娜是我的小跟班，不過她太懶散了，太懶散了，以至於艾妮塔老師時常毒打她，艾妮塔老師偶爾也毒打我，（秘密的）你知道的，只有特定的幾天。海倫娜，你應該聽艾妮塔老師的話。

艾：我沒有權利表示同情，我全部的職責只是服從命令。忠誠和服從，這便是一切，忠誠是一個重要的品德，相信我。

德國社會學家吉倫（Arnold Genlen）認為「制度」會給人一種類似動物本能的行為模式，讓我們在缺乏思考的情形下產生「制式行動」，換句話說，制度以看似合理的程序，影響著我們的作為。漢娜鄂蘭（Hannah Arendt）在其重要著作《邪惡的平庸》中，也點出了「盲從」與「無能思考」的後果。果真無能為力嗎？還是以為沉默可換取「駝鳥式的安全」？劇本出現了這樣的對話：

阿：碧娜，妳怎麼可以如此坦然？

碧：在可以抗議的時候我並沒有發聲，現在只能接受。

阿：任何處置妳都可以接受？

碧：沒有更慘了，我待過集中營，看過兒子為了麵包可以將爸爸活活打死，看著為了讓自己不被槍打到而狂奔到將人踏死，活著跟死了也沒有太大的差別。

阿：看來集中營氣氛經營得不錯。

碧：是的。

好沉重的一句回答，是的。這個世界未必美好，然而沉默會助長暴力嗎？劇場裡尖銳的提問，就像社會學提供的清晰視野，適時給了我們一個看見與反省的機會。身為一名觀眾、一個文本的閱讀者，此刻嘗試用個人的解讀，詮釋《穢土天堂》。

前言

文／鍾伯淵

《穢土天堂》初始的靈感是二○一一年四月時聽到巴奈與那布合唱的〈也許有一天〉，霎時間連結到高中時被政府徵收那位於北投半山腰的家，高中住宿的我回到那個住了十幾年的房子前，告別的機會都沒有，只剩下如殼般的廢墟，家的回憶被蕩然抹去；至今父母在北投搬過三次家，我一次都沒有幫忙過，越加鮮少回去那個父母親在的住所，或許在我高中時，靈魂並未跟隨搬離。

葬在竹林和我征戰山頭、以一敵五的小馬骨骸依舊在那，而另一隻「Lucky」則追著搬家車往山下衝，自此消失，我詫異於父母的薄情，爾

後又聽母親抑然的說她夢見Lucky變得乾淨又漂亮，不斷搖著尾巴狀似道別；家的根從底下被剷除，連父母也無措。

失根的我聽到〈也許有一天〉時，終於知道自己遺失的是什麼了，是以家為核心向外拓展的那片土地，那有各種蟲子、蛇、鳥和一堆蚊子，夏夜一家在外泡茶，前後門開著便有涼風習習，夜有蟲鳴，往登山步道走去能略避光害窺得一方星空，前望則有關渡平原及台北夜景，家從來都不是一個房屋的概念，而是空間及其回憶的整體。

遷離至今已十六年，被徵收的土地依然是一片荒蕪，少子化根本支撐不起一所小學，我仍不時地回到那被圍籬圍起的「家」撿拾我早已破碎的靈魂，試圖釐清是誰造成我原鄉的消滅，所謂國家是否具有所謂的「絕對」，近乎殘暴的巨輪又能如何抵禦。

穢土天堂的劇情合著華格納強大的音樂性中編寫，故事發展如同直球般有著絕對的必然性，近乎殘暴的壓碾著劇中角色，時至今日當我拿起劇

本翻讀依然感到其巨大的壓迫感，身為創作者也誠然感受到「穢土天堂」自身的生命力，那憑依在我身上更難以言說的歷史。

二○一一年夏天，首次去非華語系國家，也是第一次一個人出國，兩個多月間所有感官歷經劇烈震盪卻苦無人說，只能不斷在心中低迴，這段期間看了慕尼黑「達浩」、柏林「薩克森豪斯」、和波蘭「奧斯威辛」三大集中營與相關博物館，抑鬱心情依然無人能說，眼眶打轉的悲傷或是被滿屋子頭髮逼退的震驚都只能自己消化，文獻紀錄的沈重怎樣都難以寫入劇中，因此除了一段阿道夫提及集中營如何對付「地下人」的獨白有所引用外，剩餘只能放下。

所以「穢土天堂」是因為受二戰納粹歷史所震撼所寫的嗎？從劇情文體上來看的確有若干之處，但其實更多是來自生活，二○一一前後的土地正義問題、原住民相關法條問題、文化侵略……以及我的生命經驗；憑藉著「穢土天堂」我更想展現的是一個絕對的暴力，不論它有多正確也必然

有其謬誤，而我們面對如此巨輪的碾壓，也如同劇終的寓言，是否，有一天我們有停下它、改變它的可能？

《穢土天堂》

在這個世界上有某一個國家，那裡有兩批人，分別居住在地上與地下，久遠前戰敗而潛入地下的人們，成為這個國家的詭異傳說，再沒有人真正的看過他們，而在百年之後，終於有了第一位從地下世界回來的少年——阿道夫。

阿道夫：從地下世界歷劫歸來的第一個倖存者，而後被地上世界長官們提拔，成為主導開發地下世界的領導者。

艾妮塔：在教育相關部門工作，並被指派為地下人教化訓練的負責人，用以使地下人與地上人一致，方便進行政令宣導及推廣。

碧　娜：地下人；因為拯救掉落地下世界的阿道夫，而被從集中營帶出，

誠為宣導用地下人，生性被動、逆來順受。

莎　夏：地下人；宣導用地下人，不再沈溺於過去，積極融入地上社會。

海倫娜：地下人；最年幼的一位宣導用地下人，時常想家、愛哭而常被艾

妮塔教訓。

長官們：地上世界的決策高層。

（下文中楷體字表示以「錄音」方式呈現）

（燈光漸亮，三位女子和男人的區塊分別亮起，相較於女子燈區，男子的燈光始終昏暗不明。女子談話以錄音用著完美的節奏進行著，背景則是如同華格納厚重複雜的音樂；三位女子擺出制式而合乎禮儀的姿態和動作，細看三人開口前甚至連呼吸和閉眼的時機都一致。阿道夫咬著棒棒糖。）

莎：大家好，我是莎夏。

海：我是海倫娜。

碧：我是碧娜。

莎：這就叫重見天日嗎？

海：如同在黑暗的甬道重新尋獲真理。

莎：我相信在座的各位必定對我們重回地上，接受文化社會陶冶的改變感到十分驚奇。

海、碧：可不是嘛。

海：一開始我們並不瞭解禮儀。

碧：美學。

莎：和社會規範。

海：還記得剛回到地上，我腦中的辭彙庫裡並沒有請、謝謝、對不起和再見這樣的辭彙。所以在學習禮儀的時候，常常以為再見就是謝謝。

（海倫娜手上的筆掉落地板，莎夏替海倫娜撿起。）

莎：妳要跟我說？

海：謝謝。

莎：我還以為妳還改不掉妳的壞習慣。

碧：如果海倫娜又忘記了真該打屁股了。

莎：我想這就是教育的意義。

碧：打屁股嗎？

（阿道夫燈區微亮，阿道夫咬著棒棒糖發出聲響。）

莎：當然不是，我們接受全人教育開化過程中，愛是首要學習的重點，對

我們不曾學習的過失加以包容並且諄諄教化、指正。自重而後受尊重是我們教育的方針，也很快就瞭解遵守規範的必要性，因此在我們理解的前提下維持自身良好的規範與準則，使達到教育的目的。

海：因此針對我們接受某些非人道對待、令人驚恐的流言蜚語是有必要略作澄清的。

莎：否則就太對不起一路支持我們，給予我們諸多奧援的阿道夫先生了。

（三人微笑頷首看向阿道夫方向。阿道夫咬著棒棒糖發出聲響。）

碧：謠言止於智者。

海：我們就此打住。

莎：今天我們談藝術。

碧：何謂藝術？

海：如果要我說，藝術是人類文明的結晶。

莎：但更多時候我認知是人類靈魂的結晶。

碧：以美術為例。

海：美術有著悠久的歷史。從人類一出現就開始了美術史。

莎：原始社會時期人類就會在岩壁上描繪動物和狩獵的圖案，隨著文明的發展，最早的文字也是從圖畫中演變出來的，美術是一種精神產物，歷史上一直是和宗教聯繫在一起的，然隨著技術的進步，繪畫材料的發展，藝術家不斷追求更加逼真地描繪對象，美術的水平不斷發展。

海：當然隨著美術在社會的作用以及美術的地位和美術理論的發展，美術本身也不斷地變化。

碧：因此美術史研究、美術作品的內容、其在時間和空間的位置以及觀眾對作品的看法。美術作品的風格聯繫以及其歷史關聯被看作是每部作品的產生前提，在討論一個作品時必須將這個前提條件結合討論。

莎：因此我們相信不論是古典主義。

碧：或是新古典主義。

海：寫實。

碧：非寫實。

莎：現實。

海：超現實。

莎：田園。

莎、海、碧：自然、抽象、達達、野獸。

莎：都是經由時間長河所淘洗而出的美麗鑽石。藉由一顆顆璀璨光輝的鑽石及其完美的折射中窺探生命的真義。

海：藝術離我們並不遠，透過教育、透過自身感知，使我們在色彩中找到與靈魂相之呼應的感人片刻，徹底激勵我們永無止境的追尋美即生活的生活態度。

碧：相信諸位必定想問「地下」是否有藝術、有美、有教育。

莎：十分遺憾的是，沒有。因此我們萬分感激——阿道夫先生。

穢土天堂

穢土天堂

（莎、海、碧三人微笑頷首並以手擺向阿道夫方向。阿道夫咬著棒棒糖發出聲響。）

海：以及令我們得以重拾生命真諦的艾妮塔女士。

（艾妮塔出現在某一個角落。莎、海、碧三人微笑頷首看向艾妮塔。）

碧：作為教育當局最高指導人，艾妮塔女士的身教總使我們獲益良多。

莎：因此針對我們接受某些非人道對待、令人驚恐的流言蜚語是有必要略作澄清的。

碧：謠言止於智者。

海：我們就此打住。

莎：今天我們談藝術。猶記得第一次參觀達文西「蒙娜麗莎的微笑」（三人做出蒙娜麗莎的微笑動作。）這幅畫時，那一抹微笑深深烙印在我眼中、如同晶瑩剔透的水晶投入我的心湖漾起一陣陣漣漪；數百年前的神態與微笑在今日與我相遇，彷若存在數百年之久只為了剎那交

海：對我而言令我印象最深刻的一幅畫莫過於孟克的「吶喊」（三人做出
吶喊的動作），那巨大而又空洞的眼窩和嘴；彷彿吸人的深穴，將人
所有不安與驚慌全都帶入後卻又加以擴大迸射而出，無聲的吶喊瞬間
卻又嘈雜的令人難以忍受。

（燈光漸暗）

碧：「星空」；梵谷的「星空」，記得我第一次看就潸然淚下⋯⋯。

（燈暗，三人移動到舞台其他區塊；燈亮時錄音音效再進。）

莎：大家好，我是莎夏。

海：我是海倫娜。

碧：我是碧娜。

莎：我相信在座各位必定對我們重回到地上，接受文化社會陶冶的改變感
到十分驚奇。

會。

海：如同在黑暗的甬道重新尋獲真理。

莎：這就叫重見天日嗎？

海、碧：可不是嘛。

海：一開始我們並不瞭解禮儀。

碧：美學。

莎：和社會規範。

海：還記得剛回到地上，我腦中的辭彙庫裡並沒有請、謝謝、對不起和再見這樣的辭彙。所以在學習禮儀的時候，常常以為再見就是謝謝。

（海倫娜手上的筆掉落地板，莎夏替海倫娜撿起。）

莎：妳要跟我說？

海：謝謝。

莎：我還以為妳還改不掉妳的壞習慣。

碧：如果海倫娜又忘記了真該打屁股了。

莎：我想這就是教育的意義。

碧：打屁股嗎？

（阿道夫燈區微亮，阿道夫咬著棒棒糖發出聲響。）

莎：當然不是，我們接受全人教育開化過程中，愛是首要學習的重點，對我們不曾學習的過失加以包容並且諄諄教化、指正。自重而後受尊重是我們教育的方針，也很快就瞭解遵守規範的必要性，因此在我們理解的前提下維持自身良好的規範與準則，使達到教育的目的。

海：因此針對我們接受某些非人道對待、令人驚恐的流言蜚語是有必要略作澄清的。

莎：否則就太對不起一路支持我們，給予我們諸多奧援的阿道夫先生了。

（三人微笑頷首看向阿道夫方向。阿道夫咬著棒棒糖發出聲響。）

碧：謠言止於智者。

海：我們就此打住。

莎：今天我們談藝術。

碧：何謂藝術？

海：如果要我說，藝術是人類文明的結晶。

莎：但更多時候我認知是人類靈魂的結晶。

碧：以美術為例。

海：美術有著悠久的歷史。從人類一出現就開始了美術史。

莎：原始社會時期人類就會在岩壁上描繪動物和狩獵的圖案，隨著文明的發展，最早的文字也是從圖畫中演變出來的，美術是一種精神產物，歷史上一直是和宗教聯繫在一起的，然隨著技術的進步，繪畫材料的發展，藝術不斷追求更加逼真地描繪對象，美術的水平不斷發展。

海：當然隨著美術在社會的作用以及美術的地位和美術理論的發展，美術本身也不斷地變化。

碧：因此美術史研究、美術作品的內容、其在時間和空間的位置以及觀眾

對作品的看法。美術作品的風格聯繫以及其歷史關聯被看作是每部作品的產生前提，在討論一個作品時須將這個前提條件結合討論。

莎：因此我們相信不論是古典主義。

碧：或是新古典主義。

海：寫實。

碧：非寫實。

莎：現實。

海：超現實。

莎：田園。

莎、海、碧：自然、抽象、達達、野獸。

莎：都是經由時間長河所淘洗而出的美麗鑽石。藉由一顆顆璀璨光輝的鑽石及其完美的折射中窺探生命的真義。

海：藝術離我們並不遠，透過教育、透過自身感知，使我們在色彩中找到

與靈魂相之呼應的感人片刻，徹底激勵我們永無止境的追尋美即生活的生活態度。

碧：相信諸位必定想問「地下」是否有藝術、有美、有教育。

莎：十分遺憾的是，沒有。因此我們萬分感激—阿道夫先生。

（莎、海、碧三人微笑頷首並以手擺向阿道夫方向。阿道夫咬著棒棒糖發出聲響。）

海：以及令我們得以重拾生命真諦的艾妮塔女士。

（艾妮塔出現在某一個角落。莎、海、碧三人微笑頷首看向艾妮塔。）

碧：作為教育當局最高指導人，艾妮塔女士的身教總使我們獲益良多。

莎：因此針對我們接受某些非人道對待、令人驚恐的流言蜚語是有必要略作澄清的。

碧：謠言止於智者。

海：我們就此打住。

莎：今天我們談藝術。猶記得第一次參觀達文西「蒙娜麗莎的微笑」（三

（人做出蒙娜麗莎的微笑動作）這幅畫時，那一抹微笑深深烙印在我眼

中、如同晶瑩剔透的水晶投入我的心湖漾起一陣陣漣漪；數百年前的

神態與微笑在今日與我相遇，彷若存在數百年之久只為了剎那交會。

海：對我而言令我印象最深刻的一幅畫莫過於孟克的「吶喊」（三人做出

吶喊的動作），那巨大而又空洞的眼窩和嘴；彷彿吸入人的深穴，將人

所有不安與驚慌全都帶入後卻又加以擴大迸射而出，無聲的吶喊瞬間

卻又嘈雜的令人難以忍受。

（燈光漸暗）

碧：「星空」；梵谷的「星空」，記得我第一次看就潸然淚下……。

（燈暗，三人再度移動到其他區塊，三人談話錄音音效響起。）

莎：大家好，我是莎夏。

（碧娜抽離場景。）

海：我是海倫娜。

碧：我是碧娜。

碧：我們是展示品；碧娜？在母神的肚腹裡時我根本不叫這個名字；當我們被抓到地上界，一開始只有編號，所有人必須列隊等待代表自己的號碼被叫到，然後被分發到不同的地方做勞動，或是……。

莎：我相信在座各位必定對我們重回到地上，接受文化社會陶冶的改變感到十分驚奇。

海：如同在黑暗的甬道重新尋獲真理。

莎：這就叫重見天日嗎？

海、碧：可不是嘛。

海：一開始我們並不瞭解禮儀。

碧：美學。

莎：和社會規範。

碧：一開始我們並不需要禮儀、美學和社會規範。只要親暱的磨磨額頭，發出幾個嗚叫的聲音，並且深深的沉浸在其中。（碧娜發出幾個空泛、如同鯨豚一般的嗚叫聲，回到座位繼續配合錄音動作。）

海：還記得剛回到地上，我腦中的辭彙庫裡並沒有請、謝謝、對不起和再見這樣的辭彙。所以在學習禮儀的時候，常常以為再見就是謝謝。

（海倫娜手上的筆掉落地板，莎夏替海倫娜撿起。）

莎：妳要跟我說？

海：謝謝。

（海倫娜接過筆後定住不動，接著慢慢離開三人談話區塊。錄音持續播放。）

海：請、謝謝、對不起，請、謝謝、對不起。……還有再見。我會努力記得，我會努力記得。什麼是請？請是拜託，所以要拜求他們放過我的時候，我要說請放過我、請放過我、請放過我。

艾：要優雅。

海：要優雅地說請放過我。

艾：說話要清楚，這是我們約定好的不是嗎？

海：謝謝，請放過我。

艾：不，是「對不起，請放過我」；況且我們約定好的，犯錯是不是就得有個小提醒。

海：我知道了，對不起，請放過我。

艾：張開嘴巴。（海倫娜以哀求的眼神看著艾妮塔；艾妮塔用極為親切且溫柔的語氣。）張開嘴巴。（艾妮塔將棍子插進海倫娜的嘴巴用力翻攪）

艾：說話必須要清楚，談吐必須要有理，知道嗎？（艾妮塔抽出棍子後用鞋底抹了一下，海倫娜不斷乾嘔和咳嗽。）我的小淑女，這時候要說什麼呢？

海：謝謝。

艾：很好。

（艾妮塔回到在錄音介紹到艾妮塔時的狀態，海倫娜回到座位繼續動作。）

莎：我還以為妳還改不掉妳的壞習慣。

碧：如果海倫娜又忘記了真該打屁股了。

莎：我想這就是教育的意義。

碧：打屁股嗎？

（阿道夫燈區微亮，阿道夫咬著棒棒糖發出聲響。）

莎：當然不是，我們接受全人教育開化過程中，愛是首要學習的重點，對我們不曾學習的過失加以包容並且諄諄教化、指正。自重而後受尊重是我們教育的方針，也很快就瞭解遵守規範的必要性，因此在我們理解的前提下維持自身良好的規範與準則，使達到教育的目的。

海：因此針對我們接受某些非人道對待、令人驚恐的流言蜚語是有必要略

作澄清的。

莎：否則就太對不起一路支持我們，給予我們諸多奧援的阿道夫先生了。

（三人微笑頷首看向阿道夫方向。阿道夫咬著棒棒糖發出聲響。）

碧：謠言止於智者。

海：我們就此打住。

莎：今天我們談藝術。

碧：何謂藝術？

海：如果要我說，藝術是人類文明的結晶。

莎：但更多時候我認知是人類靈魂的結晶。

碧：以美術為例。

海：美術有著悠久的歷史。從人類一出現就開始了美術史。

莎：原始社會時期人類就會在岩壁上描繪動物和狩獵的圖案，隨著文明的

海：發展，最早的文字也是從圖畫中演變出來的，美術是一種精神產物，歷史上一直是和宗教聯繫在一起的，然隨著技術的進步，繪畫材料的發展，藝術家不斷追求更加逼真地描繪對象，美術的水平不斷發展。

海：當然隨著美術在社會的作用以及美術的地位和美術理論的發展，美術本身也不斷地變化。

碧：因此美術史研究、美術作品的內容、其在時間和空間的位置以及觀眾對作品的看法。美術作品的風格聯繫以及其歷史關聯被看作是每部作品的產生前提，在討論一個作品時必須將這個前提條件結合討論。

莎：因此我們相信不論是古典主義。

碧：或是新古典主義。

海：寫實。

碧：非寫實。

莎：現實。

海：超現實。

莎：田園。

莎、海、碧：自然、抽象、達達、野獸。

莎：都是經由時間長河所淘洗而出的美麗鑽石。藉由一顆顆璀璨光輝的鑽石及其完美的折射中窺探生命的真義。

海：藝術離我們並不遠，透過教育、透過自身感知，使我們在色彩中找到與靈魂相之呼應的感人片刻，徹底激勵我們永無止境的追尋美即生活的生活態度。

碧：相信諸位必定想問「地下」是否有藝術、有美、有教育。

莎：十分遺憾的是，沒有。因此我們萬分感激—阿道夫先生。

（莎、海、碧三人微笑頷首並以手擺向阿道夫方向。阿道夫咬著棒棒糖發出聲響。）

海：以及令我們得以重拾生命真諦的艾妮塔女士。

（艾妮塔出現在某一個角落。莎、海、碧三人微笑頜首看向艾妮塔。）

碧：作為教育當局最高指導人，艾妮塔女士的身教總使我們獲益良多。

莎：因此針對我們接受某些非人道對待、令人驚恐的流言蜚語是有必要略作澄清的。

碧：謠言止於智者。

海：我們就此打住。

莎：今天我們談藝術。猶記得第一次參觀達文西「蒙娜麗莎的微笑」（三人做出蒙娜麗莎的微笑動作）這幅畫時，那一抹微笑深深烙印在我眼中、如同晶瑩剔透的水晶投入我的心湖漾起一陣陣漣漪；數百年前的神態與微笑在今日與我相遇，彷若存在於數百年之久只為了剎那交會。

海：對我而言令我印象最深刻的一幅畫莫過於孟克的「吶喊」（三人做出吶喊的動作），那巨大而又空洞的眼窩和嘴；彷彿吸人的深穴，將人所有不安與驚慌全都帶入後卻又加以擴大迸射而出，無聲的吶喊瞬間

穢土天堂

041

卻又嘈雜的令人難以忍受。

（燈光漸暗）

碧：「星空」；梵谷的「星空」，記得我第一次看就潸然淚下……。

（碧娜再度脫離。）

碧：「星空」；梵谷的「星空」，記得我第一次看就潸然淚下，一片又黑又深、旋轉的寧靜夜空；一顆顆亮點點綴在旋轉的黝黑中，讓我想起一條條長長的隧道，往前看去隧道兩旁的人家門口微弱的光，和不時傳來幽微的迴響。

（燈暗）

（燈亮，音樂錄音持續播放，只剩莎夏一個人在努力做著動作一邊和海倫娜說話，海倫娜則默默地坐在一旁玩著裙襬，兩人不斷重複對話。）

莎：海倫娜，妳應該要聽艾妮塔老師的話。

海：如果我寧願被打死呢？

莎：那妳最好不要來找我求救。

（另一區燈光亮。長官與艾妮塔。）

長：地下世界探索開發的案子還在進行中，民間質疑的聲浪卻變得這麼大；艾妮塔，我想身為教育單位最高層的的妳應該親自調教這些未開化的地下人，在最短的時間使她們行禮如儀。

艾：（面有難色）我知道；但是總理大人，聽說她們具有攻擊性這一點及溝通能力都令我有所疑慮。

長：艾妮塔，沒想到妳會被誇大不實的媒體報導給唬住。

艾：是。

長：倘若她們是野獸，那就該用野獸的教育方式。

艾：野獸的教育方式？

長：（給艾妮塔棒子）我命令妳在最短時間內給我最佳成效，無論用哪一種教育手段。以地上社會人的名譽發誓；阿道夫在這一點做得很好。

長：以優良的地上社會人血統發誓……我會做得比阿道夫好。

（艾妮塔闖進莎夏和海倫娜區塊，開始毆打海倫娜，莎夏依舊重複說著「海倫娜，妳應該要聽艾妮塔老師的話。」；海倫娜吃痛開始在場上逃竄，不過艾妮塔緊追不捨。）

莎：現在是剛被阿道夫先生挑選出來的頭幾天；阿道夫先生告訴我們作為展示用地下人，我們深具潛力與內涵，所以地上社會政府對我們施行重點教育課程和禮儀訓練，展現地底人在地上一切舉止依然合乎儀禮。

海倫娜，妳應該聽艾妮塔老師的話。

艾：我沒有權利表示同情，我全部的職責只是服從命令。忠誠和服從，這

便是一切。忠誠是一個重要的品德，相信我！

莎：艾妮塔女士厭惡我們頂撞她，她總是神經兮兮的，只要我們一亂動就會引得她尖聲亂叫，以為我們會攻擊她。海倫娜，妳應該聽艾妮塔老師的話。

艾：我總是虔誠而投入地執行任務，也始終為自己屬於地上社會的高貴人種而感到驕傲，感到有價值……。

莎：海倫娜是我的小跟班，不過她就是太懶散了，（看著海倫娜與艾妮塔）太懶散了；以至於艾妮塔老師時常毒打她，（秘密的）妳知道的，只在特定的幾天。海倫娜，你應該聽艾妮塔老師的話。

艾：我沒有權利表示同情，我全部的職責只是服從命令。忠誠和服從，這便是一切。忠誠是一個重要的品德，相信我！

莎：一開始艾妮塔老師並不打人，所以我們進步很慢；不過自從阿道夫先

生介入教育課程，艾妮塔女士變得焦慮；所以她學會使用棒子，並且

越來越上手，我們進步的速度也變快了。

（海倫娜逃到莎夏旁邊）

海：莎夏，求求妳救我。

莎：莎夏！

莎、海：（頓）野獸沒有愛、野獸沒有規矩；使用鞭子、使用最鐵血的

愛。而哀號是最受教的回應。

（兩人回復至錄音段落的動作。阿道夫將碧娜帶進來，莎夏和碧娜互看一

眼而後別開視線。）

阿：這是碧娜。

（莎夏離開座位在場中遊走，碧娜加入海倫娜的錄音動作中。）

莎：阿道夫先生。

阿：妳們的新夥伴。

莎：阿道夫先生，您看我是否具有地上社會人的特質了呢？

阿：我需要你們互相勉勵。

莎：阿道夫先生，這樣是否夠優雅？

艾：阿道夫，這樣隨便帶人來難道不用顧慮訓練週期和限期展示的問題嗎？

阿：我想既然有教育專家在這，再多一個應該無妨，艾妮塔。

莎：阿道夫先生，您有我就夠了！我不會令您失望的。

艾：阿道夫你是在扯我後腿嗎？

阿：艾妮塔，首先這個教育展示計畫是由地下開發部和教育部合作；再者，僅有兩人作為示範展示……總理大人覺得太少了。還是妳需要我代妳向長官們傳達一聲「艾妮塔工作超量，恐怕無法負荷」的口信。

艾：不需要，身為教育專家的我並沒有這方面的問題。

阿：祝妳順利，艾妮塔。

（阿道夫離場，艾妮塔恨恨地看著阿道夫。）

莎：那是最後一個好日子—碧娜來的那天。

（空襲警報音效，眾人驚恐隨即做起動作，錄音開始發生狀況，三人結結巴巴的試圖接上或補充錄音所缺漏的。艾妮塔開始唸起動作指令，越來越快、越來越混亂，直到三人精疲力竭的倒在地上。）

艾：起來！起來！別逼我在妳們屁股綁上火箭。

（三人倒在地上不停地喘息，試圖起身、失敗而後倒下。）

艾：起來！（艾妮塔打倒在地上的莎夏，莎夏便爬起來滿場跑並且邊做禮儀動作，然後再度力竭倒地。再來是碧娜和海倫娜；三人在場上跑、倒下，艾妮塔也不斷地追打著三人。三人不斷求饒或說著『我不行了』等話。）

阿：艾妮塔妳的教育方式就要失敗了，除了把她們打得像亂竄的母豬外，妳什麼也沒教會她們。

艾：起來！在她們成為被教育對象前得先學會害怕疼痛。起來！母豬！

Armageddon

048

阿：希望妳的教育方針是對的！否則總理大人會非常失望的。

艾：毋庸置疑，我會替總理大人樹立最優良的地底人樣品！因為我是優越的地上社會人！（跌倒）給我起來！

阿：哈哈哈哈，我會向總理大人報告妳對於儀態教學十分講究。

艾：混帳阿道夫，這不只是我一個人的責任！我不好過，你也一樣。或許我不是你唯一的敵人，但現在我是你唯一的盟友！你最好記住這點。起來！母豬。

（阿道夫一凜，走向女子們，使用蠻力極其殘暴的──拖行代表她們的娃娃聚集一處，邊拖行邊說著，女子們亦一邊恐懼且痛苦的聚攏在一起。）

阿：要讓地底人「地上化」，得先提供健全的社會環境，然後再教育個人，這是最重要的問題。因為要讓地底人知道地上社會在文化上、經濟上，以及在政治上的種種豐功偉業，進而臣服於地上社會，非從教育著手不可。一個地底人既然為她所恐懼鞭策，那麼她們也將學會敬

畏。如果不是她明白恐懼、疼痛為何物，那又怎能對她產生敬意？

艾：教育是重要的，所以下一任內閣總理應該由教育部長擔任。

阿：我玩膩口水戰的遊戲了，既然妳是我唯一的盟友；我做到該給予的協助了，剩下就麻煩妳了。

艾：別以為你幫了一點忙我就會對你感激涕零。

阿：十二天後總理大人需要她們的「第一次陪伴」，他想跟那些先生們一起分享，既然這不方便由我來調教……麻煩妳了。

（阿道夫離場。）

艾：阿道夫！你別走！混帳。（看向三人）好了，這是第一天……我們還有十一天。

（燈暗）

（燈光漸亮中，三個女子驚恐的和艾妮塔舉止優雅站在舞台上。）

艾：讓我知道誰最適合陪伴總理大人。

莎：艾妮塔女士，或許碧娜很適合，她比我們都還要豐滿！我相信總理大人一定很喜愛。

碧：艾妮塔女士，我是不是胖了些？

艾：愚蠢的海倫娜一定不會適合陪伴總理大人，碧娜的確胖了一點，莎夏……轉圈。

莎：艾妮塔女士，我想我是不是又太瘦了？

艾：（用棒子抽打莎夏）轉身。（海倫娜轉身）看來總理大人會很滿意妳，就是妳了。

莎：艾妮塔女士，可以不要嗎？拜託！

艾：這不是我或是妳們可以決定的！誰叫妳們卑劣骯髒的身體不會得愛滋，請好好服務總理大人和其他先生們。

莎：阿道夫先生也會在場嗎？

艾：或許吧。

莎：拜託，請不要這麼做！請不要讓我做這種事。

艾：不要？妳以為妳有權利說不要？（頓）或許我會請阿道夫先生到現場監督你們有沒有確實執行這項任務。

莎：（幾乎昏厥過去）艾妮塔女士……（海倫娜和碧娜上前扶住莎夏）

海：姊姊、姊姊，妳還好嗎？

莎：（頓）艾妮塔女士，海倫娜還是處女！我想總理大人和先生們應該會非常喜歡。

海：莎夏？

艾：噢，是嗎？

莎：是的，艾妮塔女士，海倫娜比起我們更加純淨。

海：艾妮塔女士！拜託，請放過我。

艾：我們務必要求完美，三位遲早都會被總理大人和先生們召見，不如等等就讓妳們三個一起去，也省得彼此出賣……是嗎？（三人驚恐）走

吧，展現妳們在地上社會的一點點用處。

（艾妮塔帶著三位女子離開，海倫娜和莎夏走了一段距離後停下；除了莎夏和海倫娜的位置外，其他區塊燈光漸暗。）

海：莎夏姊姊，為什麼要陷害我？

莎：海倫娜，妳有過喜歡的人嗎？

海：⋯⋯⋯有。

莎：那妳應該知道在自己最喜歡的人面前被別的先生羞辱是多麼悲哀的一件事。

海：阿道夫先生嗎？

莎：是的。

海：莎夏姊姊，阿道夫先生根本就沒有把我們看在眼裡。

莎：不，只要我積極的表現和增進內涵，有一天阿道夫先生會肯定我並且真心地接受我的。

海：姊姊，妳為了一個微小的可能性，就可以出賣我，我們是一起的，不是嗎？

莎：我們當然是一起的；所以等我和阿道夫先生結為連理，我也會讓妳跟我一樣過著舒適的地上社會人生活，好嗎？

海：為了一個微乎其微的機會要犧牲掉我……我的第一次。

莎：妳的第一次？妳以為妳是誰？是在城堡上等待白馬王子的公主嗎？還是睡美人？別傻了！我們都知道自己不值錢，與其不知道被哪位先生上……不如獻給總理大人；（頓）如果妳不吭一聲的就和艾妮塔女士走，也不用連累我和碧娜；在妳唯一能派上用場的地方卻一點用處也沒有。（海倫娜哭泣，莎夏突然溫和的）別哭了，（壓著心頭）第一次會比較痛，之後就好了……之後就好了。

（燈暗）

（燈亮時，六個男人在海倫娜後方愉悅地動著，海倫娜躺在轉動的平台上。）

海：我們是行禮如儀的女子，儀禮懸掛在我們眼前、嘴邊，敬愛理性所教育我們的，充滿激進行知性探討，獲得救贖的自我辯證，獲得救贖的自我辯證。

（海倫娜露出極為驚恐的表情、痙攣，燈暗。燈亮時總理大人、先生們正在享受著海倫娜和莎夏的服務。）

總：唔！真不錯、真不錯。

A：艾妮塔說妳這個是處女呢！

總：噢！怎麼表現起來一點都不像？

（兩人笑）

A：總理大人問妳怎麼一點都不像處女。

海：因為要服侍好總理大人。

A：因為要服侍好總理大人！哈哈！

總：那妳可得好好幹才行。

A：她有辦法嗎？

總：看來是無法，那你可得好好幹！

A：是是是！總理大人我會好好幹、好好表現的。（用力且粗魯地攻擊莎夏）

總：先讓我解決手邊這個。

總：快快快，這裡等著你接手。

（阿道夫進）

阿：總理大人、先生晚安。

總：噢，我們的生力軍來了。

A：阿道夫，快去幫總理大人的忙！他忙得不可開交。

莎：阿道夫先生你……。

A：（將假陽具塞回莎夏嘴裡）繼續，別看到年輕了就想換……我的功力

可不輸一般小伙子。

總：你這傢伙真厲害！那我也不能輸你呀。（內閣總理將海倫娜翻身從後方進入，海倫娜發出慘叫。）是了！是了！這個是處女沒錯，這裡可裝不了享受。

甲：總理大人可真會開發處女地。做起事來總是劍及履及。

總：處女地，（看著自己下體）難免還是有些骯髒。阿道夫，報告進度吧。

阿：（有所顧慮的）那兩位女⋯⋯。

總：不用管她們，你說吧。

阿：是，上週開始進行的大行軍運動消耗了約莫二十五萬人，接下來會針對瞳孔顏色、髮色做分批淘汰。

總：還是太慢了。姓名部分呢？

阿：為了方便我們將原本編號的地底人加上名字，方便處理外界譴責政府

只給地底人編號的聲音，也可按照字母逐批淘汰；唯一困擾的是捏造理由使屠殺合理化。

A：屠殺地底人不需要理由。

總：今天輪到H，去去去，阿道夫，把所有名字有H的都送進大火之中或是毒氣室裡。海倫娜，妳也去、妳也去，哈哈哈。

海：總理大人請放過我！

莎：海倫娜！

A：乖乖做你該做的事。

（內閣總理從海倫娜身上離開，一手抓住海倫娜往門口走，海倫娜不停求饒。）

阿：總理大人……！

總：噓！

海：總理大人，拜託您！請不要送我進毒氣室！

總：那妳應該怎麼做。

（海倫娜默默轉身撅高屁股並將裙子往上拉）

海：我們是行禮如儀的女子，儀禮懸掛在我們眼前、嘴邊，敬愛理性所教育我們的，充滿感激進行知性探討，獲得救贖的自我辯證，獲得救贖的自我辯證。

總：很好很好！阿道夫你和艾妮塔都做得很好，教好這些母豬；接下來我要看到她們不斷地出現在電視上，裝出一副溫柔賢淑的樣子好去堵住說我們虐殺地底人、反對開發地底社會的聲浪。

A：就算我們這麼做他們也無法阻止。（A說完將陰莖往莎夏嘴裡深處塞，莎夏忍不住乾嘔了起來。）無趣。（總理和A大笑）

阿：（拿出手帕交給莎夏）擦乾淨。

莎：（感激的）阿道夫先生，謝謝。

A：真是的，有個紳士在這裡搞得我們像豺狼虎豹似的。

總：阿道夫，你可以離開了。

阿：是，祝兩位愉快。

（阿道夫離場）

Ａ：另一頭小母豬呢？

總：是不是跟其他人在另一個房間。

Ａ：我來去找他們。

總：看看他們那邊玩什麼把戲。

（總理和Ａ離開留下莎夏和海倫娜，海倫娜默默地哭泣而莎夏捏著手帕；

燈光漸暗。）

（錄音進，燈光漸進；阿道夫出現在場上。）

阿：理性有溫度，所以要用小小的熱耐心烘烤以免損壞；偶爾可以大火。女人在透明的框框內接受理性的顫動，一波波送進身體最深處的教育。來來來，只要她們學會笑、領首、理－性愛就在他們身上。

（艾妮塔領著三個女子進場，三個女子身穿囚衣。）

艾：笑！學會笑。

海：艾妮塔女士，我們真的好想睡覺。

艾：我現在不需要聽到妳的抱怨。

海：我真的好累。

艾：都閉嘴。

阿：我不認為現在是可以發表個人意見的時候。

莎：海倫娜請妳停止抱怨，我們大家都一樣。

艾：艾妮塔女士，我是⋯⋯。

穢土天堂

061

艾：（歇斯底里的）頂嘴！我不需要聽到你們頂嘴！

阿：艾妮塔，妳愛的教育呢？

艾：艾妮塔的教育？對這些低劣的對象？你指望我用什麼樣的教育？她們卑賤而危險，這正是她們被關在集中營的原因。進去！（艾妮塔指著淋浴間，三個女子開始不安的躁動。）

莎：進去？

艾：進去！

碧：進去？

海：拜託！親愛的艾妮塔女士！請不要！！

莎：那是哪裡？

海：是那些先生告訴我們的地方嗎？

莎：像傳聞中一樣、像傳聞中一樣！

碧：為什麼我們要被銷毀？

阿：艾妮塔，她們在拒絕妳的命令。

艾：進去！

阿：（輕蔑的）艾妮塔，她們想反抗妳。

艾：（幾近瘋狂的邊推邊打三個女子）進去！！

（三個女子被艾妮塔推擠，莎夏和碧娜分別往不同地方逃開，海倫娜被推入淋浴間。）

艾：阿道夫，我恨這些地底女人。她們令我從生理上感到厭惡，一看見那些變態的低劣人種的嘴臉，我的胃裡就感覺噁心。而且她們是那麼喜歡抱成一團、互相庇護！正因為神遺棄她們，所以她們不會得愛滋，連神都不屑懲罰他們，放任她們恣意又敗德的在地底下瘋狂交媾。

（燈光變化，三個女子光區亮，女子們極為驚恐地發出絕望的哀嚎，阿道夫和艾妮塔保持狀態。）

碧：脫衣服時，應在盡可能平靜的氣氛下進行，小孩子通常會哭，因為這

樣脫衣服很奇怪，但是等媽媽或地上社會收屍隊員安慰過後就會乖乖進毒氣室，拿著玩具，互相玩鬧，數以百計正值青春年華的男女，全都不疑有他走進毒氣室裡送死。外頭就是盛開的果樹，在生命中又帶有死亡的一幕。在毒殺過後，便強迫其他地底人把屍體搬上卡車，並用臨時的鐵路線載往大土坑。

莎：有人在喊叫，地上社會人喊著，「快點……。」地底人被喝令脫去衣物，被迫走往建築中更裡頭的房間，說是要讓他們沖澡，你能想像孩童一家人的遭遇嗎？他們想著……他們不知如何是好，用指甲刮著牆壁。哭天喊地，直到毒氣生效為止，當一切停止後，他們把門打開，那些二小時前還看到他們走進去的人，這會兒全都站得直直，有些人被毒氣弄得發黑發紫，無路可逃，全都死了。

海：毒氣經過三到十五分鐘就會起作用，經過一段時間之後毒氣排放的時間被縮短了。但為了一天解決一萬兩千個地底人，於是就增加劑量。

剛生下來的嬰兒只要幾分鐘就夠了；把他們拖出來的時候，有些渾身都變成詭異的螢光藍；不過有時候打開毒氣室的時候，有可能有些人還沒有真正死掉，有些人比別人更能抵抗毒氣的作用，有時候那些小地底人比大人更耐得住老鼠藥的毒氣。

（靜默）

莎、海、碧：那些沒死掉的人—包括孩子—也和屍體一起丟進焚化爐！！

（莎夏和碧娜說完話如同被吸入般急速進入淋浴間，三人極驚恐的在狹小的空間中亂竄、喊叫直到阿道夫將手舉起來三人靜默。）

阿：打開。

（蓮蓬頭水傾瀉而下，三人呆若木雞。）

阿、艾：每個人都尊敬我，我是個重要的人物。

（燈光變化，三個女子離開淋浴間前往想像的地下世界，蓮蓬頭水持續流瀉，阿道夫出現在舞台上。）

阿：我們也讓集中營的囚犯感染葡萄球菌、氣性壞疽菌、破傷風以及混合培植的幾種致病細菌，目的是研究磺胺類藥物的治療作用。我們具體操作卻從不進行任何真正負責任的監控。在囚犯毫不知情的情況下，使他們的腿部下端受到感染。當少數倖存者的傷口出現癒合的疤痕時，傷口常常會被深深切開直至露出骨骼。除了往傷口植入細菌組織之外，還常常會加入木屑和玻璃渣。受試者的腿部很快開始化膿。為了觀察情況發展的過程，不會對受害者進行任何治療，他們往往極其痛地死去……每一個系列的實驗都將重複至少六次，會使用六至十個年輕女性──通常選的都是最漂亮的。並且對地底人進行永久絕育的手術，可行的辦法是採用足量的Ｘ光射線，從而進行閹割並產生一系列相關後果。大量的Ｘ光線會摧毀卵巢或者睪丸的內分泌能力……但是由於不可能用鉛板罩住周圍的組織，我們必須承認一個棘手的問題，那就是這些器官將會被摧毀，隨之而來的是Ｘ射線所謂的『副作

用』帶來的影響。經過射線過度照射，在接下來的幾天或幾個星期之內，受到照射的皮膚部位將出現燒傷。比如，一個很可行的辦法是把試驗者叫到一個櫃台前面，讓他在那裡站大約三分鐘，回答些問題，或者填寫表格。櫃台後面的辦事員就可以按按鈕啟動放射線儀器，使兩根 X 光管道同時射出射線，這是因為射線必須同時從兩邊進行照射。通過這種辦法，利用一種雙管道放射儀器，一天內可以對一百五十至兩百人進行絕育，如果有二十套這樣的儀器，一天就可以解決三千至四千人……至於幾週或者幾個月之後，那些人將發現自己被絕育，這是無關緊要的。

（在地下世界中，三人隨著音樂使用各種不同姿勢擁抱，輕聲哼著『家』的不規則音直到音樂結束，燈暗；蓮蓬頭水持續流瀉直到下一場燈亮。）

（燈亮，阿道夫正在整理文件，艾妮塔進。）

艾：恭喜我們的第一百場對外展示和電視節目通告。

阿：（頭也不抬的）嗯。

艾：很多文件需要整理嗎？

阿：（依然整理文件）是。

艾：忙什麼？

阿：善後。

艾：善後？我以為你為了開發地底能源會忙的焦頭爛額；總理大人應該交代你不少工作吧？

阿：（終於抬起頭）艾妮塔妳來我這究竟有什麼事呢？

艾：沒什麼，特意過來關心你。

阿：明人不說暗話。

艾：阿道夫你永遠都這麼不為所動！我是來看總理大人是不是將地底人樣

阿：品交給你處理。

阿：沒有。

艾：沒有，那就是說自從一個多月前展示地底人的活動已經徹底暫停了？

阿：是。

艾：他們不需要使用展示地底人漂白整個地下世界開發計畫嗎？

阿：展示地底人已經過度曝光了，人民對她們已經失去興趣。

艾：所以地底人已經過度曝光了，人民對她們已經失去興趣。

阿：除了開發進度的例行彙報。

艾：所以這一個月來你都沒有和總理大人碰面。

阿：沒有。

艾：所以總理大人也沒有再找她們進去「服務」他和其他先生們。

阿：沒有。

艾：所以地底人熱潮過了？

阿：我想是的。

艾：批判地下世界開發的人卻越來越多？

阿：艾妮塔，妳不是教育學者嗎？怎麼反倒像個學生一樣拼命問問題。

艾：你不擔心熱潮一過就會失勢？

阿：我所要做的就是確實執行命令，沒有別的。

艾：阿道夫、阿道夫，你是真的這麼不為所動。（艾妮塔轉身離開）難怪你可以成為地底人口中的殺人惡魔。

（艾妮塔下；阿道夫停止手邊動作，陷入某種曖昧不明的情緒中。碧娜出

現在阿道夫房間內，莎夏則是不停的在四周遊走。）

碧：阿道夫先生，您找我嗎？

阿：嗯，你們最近好嗎？

碧：托您的福，還算可以，過了一陣子清閒的日子。

阿：海倫娜還是那麼神經質嗎？

碧：（斟酌的）海倫娜比較不習慣服務先生們。

阿：所以妳和莎夏很適應？

碧：如果我們別無選擇，那我們也只能適應。

阿：很多事情都沒有選擇的權利。

碧：是。

阿：（頓）那妳怎麼想，關於妳和莎夏。

碧：我知道她十分欣賞阿道夫先生。

阿：即使我這樣對你們？

（下面莎夏台詞碧娜亦說，但音量極小。）

莎：阿道夫先生，我十分欣賞您的一絲不苟；不管您怎麼對我，我都知道那是您出於上級命令的無奈。

阿：或是當她正在服侍先生們時看到我？

莎：我知道您無力扭轉狀況，但您用您一絲不苟的方式愛著我……們，而非如先生般的利用、享受。阿道夫先生，我的身體可以供任何先生使用，但心裡純潔的只讓您一個人進入。

阿：老鼠只能與老鼠，狼只能與狼，狐狸只能與狐狸，鵝只能與鵝交配，以保持物種血統的純淨。絕對沒有一隻貓會愛上老鼠，地上社會人也有同樣的義務。

莎：為什麼？

碧：阿道夫先生，為什麼？

阿：為了保衛血與純淨。

碧：阿道夫先生，您真的這樣認為嗎？

阿：身為地下世界開發的最高領導人，我從來不懷疑我所說的。

碧：您所說的？那總理大人呢？

阿：這個問題超過妳的限度了。

碧：很抱歉。

（靜默，莎夏下場。）

阿：妳相信救贖嗎？

碧：什麼？

阿：妳有仇恨嗎？對地上社會？

碧：阿道夫先生，如果我們別無選擇，那我們的仇恨又能怎麼辦？

阿：復仇？

碧：那是我們全然不敢想像的事，我們要如何和整個地上社會為敵。

阿：所以妳選擇任人擺佈？會不會其實地底人的抗爭會使你們現在依然安然的活在地底。

碧：但我們被從地底挖出來了，不是嗎？

阿：（激動）挖出來的時候為什麼不掙扎?!

碧：死亡，所以我們只能和死亡一起生活。

阿：現在也是？

碧：到現在我依然感覺到死亡就在我耳邊呼氣。

阿：而我是播種死亡的農夫。

碧：您十分盡責。

阿：是，我十分盡責。

碧：（笑）大家都說「在集中營沒有神，因為這裡可怕到連神也決定不來了。」。

阿：看來我的盡責獲得空前的勝利。

碧：是的。

（靜默）

阿：莎夏恨妳嗎？因為我很常找妳來。

碧：我盡量做到不讓她恨。

阿：很困難吧？

碧：因為我們只剩彼此了。

阿：碧娜，妳怎麼可以如此坦然？

碧：在可以抗議的時候我並沒有發聲，現在只能接受。

阿：任何處置妳都可以接受？

碧：沒有更慘的了；我待過集中營，看過兒子為了麵包可以將爸爸活活打死，看著為了讓自己不被槍打到而狂奔到將人踏死，活著跟死了也沒有太大的差別。

阿：看來集中營氣氛經營得不錯。

碧：是的。

（停頓）

阿：如果我沒有找到妳？

碧：那我現在大概跟著我母親一起長眠地下。

阿：我也只能帶妳們三個出來了。

碧：我知道阿道夫先生已經違背您工作的規範了。

阿：現在這樣苟活著會恨我嗎？

碧：不，我只能專注在當下，過去和未來都不是我有能力思考的。

阿：碧娜，妳是恨我的吧？

碧：阿道夫長官，我只會想我等等一個小時可能要做的工作，愛和恨不是我所能控制的……。

阿：阿道夫長官？好，我命令妳回答我！妳恨我吧。

碧：我恨您，我恨不得將您殺了分屍，把您的頭掛在高高的旗杆上讓所有

Armageddon

076

的地底人看。

（停頓）

阿：這樣妳的仇恨就會消失嗎？

碧：不會。

（靜默）

碧：我知道這是您的工作，您只是忠實地執行；這世界上沒有壞人，只是立場不同罷了。

阿：但是妳恨我？

碧：是。

（停頓）

阿：所有地底人都唾棄我？

碧：沒錯，阿道夫先生絕對無法獲得任何地底人的原諒。

阿：即使莎夏？

碧：我相信她內心深處也在恨著您。

（停頓）

阿：永遠無法被原諒？

碧：永遠，但永遠也不代表什麼。

阿：妳回去吧。

碧：是。

（碧娜轉身離開）

阿：如果讓你們回到地下呢？

碧：阿道夫先生，魚放生到只有血的池子能活嗎？

阿：所以妳不願意回去？

碧：是回不去了。

阿：回去了……。

碧：也無法原諒。

（頓）

阿：我知道了。

碧：那我回去了。

阿：但妳知道這都是工作使然對吧？

碧：我全然瞭解。

（頓）

阿：妳和妳的家人救了摔進地洞的我。

碧：是。

阿：現在會後悔嗎？

碧：有一點；但如果沒救您，同樣的事也可能發生；很感謝至少是您。

阿：怎麼說。

碧：您總是精確地執行任務，不算太折磨人。

阿：所以稍微可被原諒一些些。

碧：千百萬分之一吧。（頓）阿道夫先生，我先離開了。

（碧娜轉身離開）

阿：謝謝。

（碧娜離場）

碧：（頭也不回的）不會。

（碧娜離場；阿道夫停在場上，燈光漸暗。）

（微亮的燈光中三個女人在狹小而冷清的房間裡來回踱步不停抽著煙，直到最後三人一起熄煙；海倫娜走到窗邊不停朝外張望，碧娜則一邊看書一邊捲著玫瑰花。）

莎：海倫娜，妳在看什麼？

海：我們已經兩個多月沒對外展示跟上節目了。

莎：這樣很好，既不用背藝術史也不用硬擠笑臉。

海：先生們也很久都沒來了。

莎：妳希望他們來嗎？

海：當然不希望。

莎：（冷笑）但妳說得好像很希望他們來；下次先生們來我會告訴他們妳很期待他們來，每天都在窗邊看呀看的。

海：（驚恐）沒有；莎夏姊姊，請不要這樣跟他們說，不然⋯⋯。

莎：不然怎麼樣？

海：不然他們又會在我身上刻日期。

碧：海倫娜，妳何不來陪我坐坐呢？

莎：碧娜，我們聊得正開心。

（莎夏和碧娜短暫對看，碧娜再度低頭看書。）

海：（看向窗外，呢喃）沒關係，我想看看外面。

莎：海倫娜，妳也可以像碧娜一樣看看書，妳看碧娜就是看了這麼多書才能靠阿道夫先生近一點，看書是好事。

海：我不喜歡，看書讓我想到艾妮塔女士的棒子……艾妮塔女士好久沒來，（頓）阿道夫先生也是。對了，碧娜，上次阿道夫先生找妳去他辦公室做什麼？

碧：沒什麼，問一些事情。

海：什麼樣的事情。

碧：瑣碎無聊的事，沒什麼好說的。

（莎夏用力從椅子上站起，假意地拖拉一下椅子；隨手拿起一本書，半丟半推地塞進海倫娜懷裡。）

莎：多嘴！別人不想說的事別問。

海：嗯。

莎：嘴巴上講同甘共苦，事實上就是有特權。

碧：（哀求的）莎夏。

海：我不需要特權，我想回去。

莎：回去？回去哪裡。

海：地下。好想吃媽媽做的烤地鼠。

莎：噁心！妳看地上社會有人在吃這道菜的嗎？真是野蠻。

海：可是真的很好吃呀。或許只是因為他們沒吃過，請他們吃吃看，或許地上社會的人會瘋狂地愛上烤地鼠。

莎：真不敢相信妳接受教育這麼久還會說這種話；野蠻，這是野蠻的表

穢土天堂

083

現。

碧：迷迭蘚白蝸牛也不錯！

海：喔！只有生日才吃得到的迷迭蘚蝸牛；每年媽媽煮的時候附近兩、三百公尺內香味瀰漫，然後大家都會帶著禮物來換一顆蝸牛。

碧：吃蝸牛能為地底人招來好運。

（頓）

海：我們一定是吃不夠多。我好想媽媽。

莎：海倫娜，妳真是軟弱地令人討厭！

碧：我們都想家。

莎：我們都知道那裡不是適合生活的地方。

碧：冬天冷到骨頭都要結冰，於是大家總是擠在火爐邊跑跑跳跳。

海：那時候好幸福。

莎：閉嘴！

（靜默）

碧：「星空」；梵谷的「星空」，記得我第一次看就潸然淚下，一片又黑
又深、旋轉的寧靜夜空；一顆顆亮點點綴在旋轉的黝黑中，讓我想起
一條條長長的隧道，往前看去隧道兩旁的人家門口微弱的光，和不時
傳來幽微的迴響。夜空的線條又像聲響又像地下特有的氣味。

海：怎麼可以不想家？

碧：記得嗎？記得嗎？離開下水道前最後一次回首，過去正在崩毀；我們
被強行從母親溫暖的子宮刨出。那是我住了十幾年的地方！那是我住
了十幾年的地方！家！家！

莎：房子再美又怎麼樣？是誰有權力這麼做，一張公告、一股勢力，完全
不看我們在地下的根就將我們拔起、不聽我們悲痛的哀號。

海：我小小的房間有一扇窗，晚上就可以聽見蟲子唏唏窣窣爬過的聲音；
還記得有一年夏天特別熱，小飛蟲好多好多，因為燈讓小飛蟲鑽過紗

窗跑到房裡，白色的牆上布滿一個個的小黑點，讓我驚慌失措地逃出房間找媽媽求救……。

（停頓，莎夏用力地將書甩在地板上。）

莎：海倫娜！太暗了，把燈轉亮些。

（海倫娜頓了一會，隨即將燈轉亮。）

莎：又開始做起白日夢了，白日夢不會讓妳的日子過得更好。再說，有電有自來水多好，不用擔心沼氣燈爆炸、也不用煩惱才剛洗好澡身上就有水腥味。

碧：我現在倒懷念起來了。

莎：碧娜，做人要向前看，我們現在是地上社會的一份子；如何做更好的地上社會人才是最實際的。（頓）海倫娜就像是我的小妹妹，怎麼可以再讓她沉浸在過去的陰影之中呢？

碧：現在生活在黑暗之中。

Armageddon

海：燈不夠亮嗎？

莎：可愛的海倫娜，那是妳不用聽懂的無聊比喻；我們只要盡本分，展現地底人最為優雅受教的一面就夠了，這是我們的工作。

碧：即使已經死了上百萬地底人。

海：「今天輪到Ｈ，去去去，阿道夫，把所有名字有Ｈ的都送進大火之中或是毒氣室裡。海倫娜，妳也去、妳也去……」。（海倫娜不停喃喃自語）

（海倫娜發出一聲短促的喊叫，隨即露出害怕的神情。）

莎：這是我們不能提的！也不再需要提起！大家都知道（頓）那是過度渲染的謊話。

碧：妳這才是謊話。

莎：那我們應該怎麼辦！對著所有地上社會人吐口水、咆哮？一年多了，這件事情也落幕了，但妳還是想把所有地上社會人逼到絕境好展現自

己所受到極大的苦痛！

碧：從來都沒有落幕的一天。

莎：（突然和緩）我不知道妳想折磨誰。（看向海倫娜）

碧：我只是不想讓自己看起來接受和平的假象。

莎：但妳就是。

碧：我們都是。

莎：笑話！碧娜，不要逼著所有人看著地底人巨大的傷口！無濟於事。我要繼續走下去，自從在集中營裡看著媽媽倒在地上的屍體後；我在地上社會，就需要照著他們的遊戲規則才得以生存。（到海倫娜旁）妳不需要回憶，如果有地下社會的回憶，那就會有逃跑時她哥哥在她面前活生生被地上社會人踏成肉泥的畫面，或是爸爸被丟在水池泡爛的畫面；海倫娜，看看妳的衣服多漂亮、妳看看，妳沒有被送到毒氣室、也沒有被丟進焚化爐，先生們是在跟妳開玩笑的，是不是？

海：是。

莎：碧娜，脫離陰溼的地下世界是幸福的，即使陽光太灼熱、太刺眼，照射十分鐘就會令我們紅腫發痛。海倫娜……妳看這個房間多明亮，多乾爽。

海：可是我的皮膚都乾裂了。

莎：妳看看外面的夕陽多美。

海：可是曬太久就會紅腫發癢。

莎：還有一打開就嘩拉嘩拉流出來的自來水。

海：自來水有一股好刺鼻的藥水味。

莎：（勃然大怒）這就是妳要過的生活！別像個小孩一樣抱怨了！妳哥在試圖逃跑的時候怎麼樣被人踏成肉泥妳忘了嗎？一覺起來時妳媽下體多了一根鐵棒死在妳旁邊妳忘了？別耍賴了！海倫娜，別以為妳是清純少女了，認份地過好現在的日子！

（海倫娜狂奔跑開，拿起一個下體被插上鐵棒的娃娃。）

海：媽媽，親愛的媽媽，妳為什麼一動也不動？昨天妳還一直叫我不要睜開眼睛、不要看、快睡、快睡！今天換妳不睜開眼睛；媽媽，摸摸我的臉看看我；我不哭，我也不會再問為什麼大家看著哥哥被踏死卻不能幫忙……。

莎：海倫娜！

海：（往莎夏方向去）媽媽，親愛的媽媽妳怎麼被插一根鐵管就死了？我之前每天晚上都有好多位先生不停地插我！他們一邊說髒卻一邊不停地插進來；媽媽，我還活著為什麼妳死了？

莎：停止妳的白日夢。

海：是的，姊姊；我要認份過好現在的生活。

碧：海倫娜。

莎：很好。

海：那我們現在做什麼？

莎：或許妳可以看看書；或許妳可以問問碧娜，也許他從阿道夫先生那邊得到一些消息沒有跟我說。

海：碧娜姊姊，阿道夫先生都跟妳說。

碧：真的沒什麼。

海：碧娜姊姊，阿道夫先生都跟妳說了什麼？

莎：所以有人當真有事不跟「自己人」說。

海：求求妳跟我們說，好多天都沒有人來找我們，拜託！請告訴阿道夫先生，我悶得慌了，整天都在做白日夢！整天都夢到他們把我小小的弟弟帕的一聲摔到地上媽媽卻不看一眼；或是去告訴阿道夫先生給我們工作。……除了看書以外。

碧：親愛的海倫娜，阿道夫並沒有跟我說什麼，也沒有任何工作可以給我們；上次我請求過他了，妳記得嗎？

海：阿道夫、阿道夫，妳就不能加個先生嗎？但是……阿道夫先生不給我

們任何工作？難道真的向那位先生說的一樣？

莎：海倫娜！妳剛說了什麼？

碧：噢，海倫娜。

莎：那位先生說了什麼？

海：上次的那位先生告訴我，阿道夫長官會把我們趕回地下。

莎：我的天呀，這不是真的！（頓）碧娜，妳知情嗎？

碧：我不是很清楚。

莎：海倫娜，那位先生為什麼這樣說？

海：那位先生說現在地上社會的人開始發現政府對地下人施暴、虐殺，焚化爐惡臭的黑煙二十四小時不停冒出來，一個焚化爐燒壞了再新蓋兩個，兩個壞了就再蓋四個……。

碧：那位先生還說「現在這樣趁了地底人的意，你們一定也很得意吧！骯髒的地底人也可以被重視，地底人也可以在地上工作；不過地上社會

才沒有這麼多工作可以給你們；準備滾回妳們的老鼠窩吧」。

海：不過先讓我再爽一下……。

莎：海倫娜，為什麼妳沒有跟我說。

海：我怕是真的，如果我說出來的話。

莎：不過妳卻跟碧娜說？

碧：我發現她這陣子怪怪的，逼問到後來海倫娜才跟我說的。

莎：海倫娜！我應該說過有事情第一個要先跟我說的！我是妳們的老大，妳忘了嗎？

海：對不起。

莎：所以阿道夫先生也跟你說了同樣的事。

碧：阿道夫先生……他沒有明說，但有稍微透露一點。

莎：你們竟然都不跟我說。

海：（哭）莎夏，對不起！我真的太害怕了，我好想回去！不過我的爸

爸、媽媽、哥哥還有小小的弟弟都不能跟我一起回去了，只有我一個人、只有我一個人能回去！我想到就好怕好怕。

莎：海倫娜，不要再哭了；（癱軟）那我們該怎麼辦？我不要回去陰暗潮濕的地下。

海：沒有爸爸幫我趕走一大片的蟑螂了。

莎：怎麼可以，阿道夫先生怎麼會允許這種事發生？我們是他最好的地底人模範呀。

碧：這一切都只是謠言，沒必要信以為真。

莎：碧娜，是這樣說的嗎？我們又不像妳一樣有阿道夫先生替妳擋著。

海：我們不像碧娜一樣？

莎：是呀；海倫娜，我們沒有得到阿道夫先生的青睞，所以我們會被送回去；但碧娜……不會。

碧：沒有、才沒有，海倫娜妳不要聽莎夏亂說。

Armageddon
094

海：那我就會被送回去只剩我一個人活著的家，我不要！好恐怖、好恐怖！碧娜姊姊，可以幫我跟阿道夫先生說不要讓我回去好嗎？拜託。

碧：這只是謠言呀，況且我也會和妳們一起被送回去。

海：我不要！我不要！

莎：阿道夫先生再也不需要地底人模範了……我們已經沒有利用價值了？不是要成功將我們改造成地上社會人嗎？不是要讓所有地上社會人看到地底人也能有素養有美德？阿道夫先生怎麼會這樣對我們？

海：（喃喃的）槍……那只好用槍。

碧：不！海倫娜。

莎：槍？海倫娜妳說什麼槍？

碧：海倫娜，不可以……求妳。

海：那位先生有給我一把槍。

碧：不。

莎：為什麼？

海：他說我們可以拿著槍去逼阿道夫先生讓我們留下。

莎：那位先生為什麼要跟妳這麼說？

碧：莎夏、海倫娜；放棄這個愚蠢的想法，拜託。

海：那位先生說所有對地底人的壞事都是阿道夫先生指使的，阿道夫先生是最高決策者；如果想留下來就得拿槍逼迫阿道夫先生，甚至⋯⋯。

莎：甚至？

碧：甚至殺了他為地底人報仇；但這不是真的，這只是地上社會人的鬥爭！我們沒必要因此讓地底人成為代罪羔羊。

莎：但我們被送回地下卻是不爭的事實。

碧：一切都還不確定呀⋯⋯！

莎：碧娜！這一次、就這一次，跟我們站在一起。

碧：我一直都跟你們站在一起。

莎：海倫娜妳也不想回地下對吧？（海倫娜點頭）那就讓我們帶著槍⋯⋯去找阿道夫先生。

（燈暗）

（燈光漸亮，阿道夫在場上來回踱步，總理帶著先生們進來。）

總：阿道夫。

（眾人應和）

阿：總理大人、各位晚安。

總：恭喜你立了大功。

阿：謝謝。

A：阿道夫真是後生可畏。

B：不是嗎？開發地下世界就算了……。

C：竟然還有辦法從地底社會找到愛滋病的解藥。

A：運氣好的時候就連躺著都能有政績。

B：阿道夫政績是躺來的呀？

（B抓了一把阿道夫的屁股，眾笑。）

阿：請問總理大人特意來訪有什麼工作要交代我嗎？

C：好聰明的小伙子。

A：是呀、是呀，無事不登三寶殿。

總：好了，別再虧這個小伙子了，他可是我最好的接班人呀。

B：哎呀呀呀！你們看看，內閣總理欽點了。

A：那我們可得客氣一點囉。

C：那個叫艾妮塔的小妮子不就沒希望了？

B：哎～是耶！

C：那總理大人不就欺負她了。

（眾笑）

總：夠了、夠了，阿道夫呀，開發地下社會目前除了愛滋解藥和疫苗研發外，新能源的開發有發展嗎？

阿：總理大人，很遺憾的，我們發現地下社會除了某些特定地點有少量的沼氣外，並沒有當初探勘預估到可能有的石油能源或貴重金屬的可能

性。

總：這樣呀。

A：總理大人，這樣就夠啦，否則地下社會開發讓阿道夫聲勢扶搖直上，功高震主呀。

阿：沒有的事，都是因為按照總理大人的指示才能有今日的成績。

C：真會說話。

B：哈哈，這小伙子果然有前途。

總：嗯。

阿：總理大人，地下社會能源探勘進度報告書明天我會呈到您桌上。

總：不用了，差不多要抽手了。

阿：您的意思是停止能源開發並且……。

B：哎唷！

C：並且？

A、B、C：並且呢。

總：阿道夫，你說看看。

阿：並且全面撤離地下社會，摧毀集中營、毒氣室，以及銷毀任何可能遭受眾議的資料。

總：聰明。

A、B、C：聰明呀！聰明呀。

阿：我會交代幾名親信進行這項工作，預計三天內完成。

總：嗯，那集中營的地底人呢？

（頓）

阿：報告總理大人，我們會建立臨時地底人安置區加以安置，並輔導他們進入……。

A、B、C：嘻嘻嘻。

A：我就說他還年輕嘛。

C：真不懂事。

總：阿道夫，集中營的地底人有辦法在三天內全部建檔嗎？

阿：目前全國各處約有上百個集中營，三天內的確有困難。

總：那如果不需要建檔呢？

（A、B、C笑。）

阿：總理大人，我不太明白您的意思。

C：我就說他還嫩嘛。

B：嘻嘻嘻，這點道理怎麼會不懂呢。

總：如果他們不存在怎麼需要建檔。

阿：報告總理大人，上百個集中營約莫有一百三十萬人……。

C：實際上集中營根本沒有任何地底人了。

B：完全沒有任何人了。

A：完全是開採初期供地底人暫住的地方。

B：中期開始就逐漸輔導地底人回歸地下了。

總：阿道夫，我十分看好你！你……不會讓我失望吧。

（A、B、C嘻嘻嘻的笑）

阿：是，集中營自中期就沒有任何地底人居住，因此我會派員進行「清掃」。

總：清掃？（笑）是呀、是呀。阿道夫，要掃乾淨呀，掃不乾淨會有灰塵；不太好，是吧？

阿：是。

總：阿道夫，垃圾你要倒哪裡呢？

阿：當初開發地底能源時在國境北方挖了一個深一・二公里的洞。

總：嗯；好好辦，結束後來找我們吃個飯。

阿：是。

（總理和其他人轉身欲離開）

總：對了，阿道夫；那三個樣品也要處理掉。

阿：但是以她們在地上社會的知名度……。

總：那就地底回歸大使的名義把她們送回去吧，聽說她們要將地上社會優良的教育和秩序帶回地底下不是嗎？

A：你有聽說過這件事嗎？

B、C：有。

A：誰說的。

B：總理大人。

（A、B、C笑）

阿：總理大人，地下社會現在可能已經不方便住人了，既然她們已經接受良好的訓練與教育，是否可以……。

總：養虎為患；這件事就這麼定了；至於回到地下社會他們還能不能活，是她們的問題。

Armageddon
───────────
104

阿：我瞭解了。

總：我們走吧。

B：嘻嘻嘻。

A：好可惜，又沒有玩具了。

B：不然你以為現在要去哪？

A、B、C：挑玩具。（回頭）阿道夫，好好辦唷。

阿：各位晚安。

（總理與A、B、C穿過阿道夫離開，隨即將衣服脫下成堆，並將偶頭放置其上，成為莎夏、海倫娜和碧娜；三人略顯緊張卻極力維持鎮定。）

莎、海、碧：阿道夫先生您好，好久不見。

（三人依序迎向阿道夫親吻他的左右臉頰）

莎：請問阿道夫先生今天特別找我們來有什麼事嗎？

阿：回去。

（眾人一愣）

莎：回去？我們才剛到呀。

阿：我說回去。

莎：阿道夫先生您在逗我們嗎？我們剛剛正在學習環境衛生……。

阿：妳不懂我的意思嗎？

海：但是阿道夫長官，我們真被您搞糊塗了……。

（阿道夫冷冷的看著三人，三人開始慌張。）

莎：阿道夫先生，請不要開這種玩笑呀。

海：我們最近正在利用新媒材進行創作，阿道夫長官，下個星期二就要開展了。

莎：是呀，我們還打算邀請阿道夫先生您擔任開幕剪綵的貴賓呢。

阿：不用了，回去吧。

莎：阿道夫先生，我們真的不知道您要我們回去哪？

海：所以您願意擔任我們展覽的開幕剪綵貴賓嗎？

阿：不需要白費心力了。

莎：離開這裡我們還能去哪裡呢？

（停頓）

碧：請阿道夫先生直接了當告訴我們您的決定吧，不要再戲弄我們了。

（停頓）

阿：地下。

（停頓）

莎：不可以！阿道夫先生您不可以這樣對我們。現在要我們回到骯髒潮濕的地底下，那我們該怎麼辦？

海：我們已經無法整天在昏黑的地方生活了。

莎：污穢的水從岩壁上的孔隙不斷滲出，老鼠隨時從身邊一竄而過；蟑螂！還有蟑螂，帶著各種噁心病菌四處散播的蟑螂在妳睡覺時爬過妳

嘴巴、試圖鑽進妳的耳朵、鼻子。

海：我光想到就沒辦法呼吸了。

莎：沒有乾淨的自來水我們要怎麼盥洗？

海：生菌數超標的水怎麼能喝？

莎：親愛的阿道夫先生，請不要這樣對我們。

海：我們該怎麼辦？

阿：這是妳們的問題。

碧：阿道夫先生，難道沒有一絲轉圜的餘地嗎？

（阿道夫看著碧娜）

阿：很遺憾的，這是最後決定。

碧：我們何時得動身。

阿：七天後會專人送你們回去。

（莎夏看著兩人，手放到自己的小提包上。）

碧：您怎麼能能這樣對我們。

阿：老鼠只能與老鼠……。

碧：狼只能與狼，狐狸只能與狐狸，鵝只能與鵝交配，以保持物種血統的純淨。

阿：絕對沒有一隻貓會愛上老鼠，地上社會人也有同樣的義務。

莎：阿道夫先生，我們知道您是有影響力的大人物；（頓）請您再做最後考慮。

（阿道夫略帶疑惑的看著莎夏）

莎：（略帶威脅的）請您鄭重考慮。

碧：（緊張的）阿道夫先生，這是我們最後的請求。

阿：（笑）很遺憾的……。

（莎夏掏出手槍）

莎：你不應該這樣對我們！

（海倫娜哭了起來）

莎：現在請您鄭重考慮，讓我們留在地上社會。

阿：（對著碧娜）這項行動妳知情？

莎：阿道夫！看著我！

碧：知道。

莎：阿道夫！看著我！

阿：妳同意了？

碧：是，我參與了。

莎：閉嘴！現在槍在我手上，你沒有發問的權利？答應我們，讓我們留下來。（阿道夫冷冷的看著莎夏；停頓。）夠了！別哭了！

（海倫娜哭聲轉小）

海：這麼做真的好恐怖。

莎：當初妳也同意的。

海：我知道。

莎：那麼妳就不該反悔。

阿：（對碧娜）妳真讓我失望。

碧：我們別無選擇。

莎：現在就去打電話，讓我們留下來。

阿：是誰提供妳們的槍的。

海：是光頭的先生。

莎：別說話。

阿：所以你們認為一把槍足以改變妳們的未來？

碧：這是我們最後、也是唯一的辦法。

莎：現在輪不到你質疑我們，如果你想活著走出去……。

阿：那就打電話？

莎：沒錯！

阿：那我應該打給誰？

莎：別問我們！你自己想！

海：如果你還要命的話，阿道夫長官。

莎：海倫娜！閉嘴。

海：海倫娜！閉嘴。

海：為什麼要我閉嘴？（向莎夏靠近）閉嘴！閉嘴！我難道不是要被送回地下世界的其中一個人嗎？

莎：不要在這個時候說這個！走開！

海：莎夏姊姊，妳以為手上有槍就可以控制一切、控制所有人，（伸手抓住槍）要求我們可以做什麼，不可以做什麼？

莎：妳在幹什麼？住手！

海：這把槍是我的那位先生給我的！也應該是我來拿。為什麼都是妳在要威風！

莎：放手！妳的那位先生？你有這麼多位先生你還記得是哪位嗎？是喜歡像狗一樣從後面上妳的那位先生，還是用電電妳陰部的那位？放手！

海：把槍給我！都是妳！我第一個晚上被不知道多少位先生上，一個接著一個！直到我完全沒有感覺、精液不斷從陰道溢出，他們還是不停地上。

莎：那不能怪我！

海：如果妳不把我的事說出來的話！

莎：那就會是我被強暴！

海：他們把水灌到我嘴裡、身體裡，然後捶打我，讓我把灌進去的水全部吐出來……流出來，好洗滌我污穢骯髒的地下人身體。然後再一次、再一次、再一次……。

莎：妳少自憐了。最後誰不是這樣被對待。

海：但妳就是把所有人看成妳的部下！沒有人懂妳，妳最高貴。自視為女王！

碧：海倫娜……。

莎：閉嘴！海倫娜，別說不合時宜的話！

海：不合時宜！所以我現在擋在妳前面，影響妳成為改革英雄了是嗎？

莎：放手！

海：我還要再說更多！因為妳得不到阿道夫才會用槍指著他。

莎：閉嘴。

海：妳忌妒碧哪比妳贏到更多阿道夫的信任！

莎：閉嘴。

海：所以妳只好不停地告狀、玩小把戲！想搞掉碧娜！不過妳都失敗了。

莎：閉嘴。

海：去當妳地底世界的女王吧！蟑螂和老鼠會很樂意親吻妳的腳指頭。

莎：閉嘴。

海：然後妳只能仰望阿道夫和碧娜兩個人相親相愛。

莎：夠了！（莎夏用力把海倫娜推倒在地。看向阿道夫。）看到我們起內

闓你很開心吧？這是你想要的吧？

阿：我沒請妳們在我面前演戲。

莎：什麼？

阿：而且還是不入流的那種。

莎：你不要以為我不敢開槍！

碧：莎夏！別忘了我們是為了什麼來的。

莎：我知道，我當然知道。給我們永遠住在地上的權利。

阿：妳有籌碼談嗎？

莎：憑你的命。

阿：我的命。

海：這個籌碼難道還不值錢嗎？那我們的革命英雄起義就要失敗了。

碧：海倫娜。

莎：我數到三，你不答應我就開槍了。

阿：莎夏，開了槍又怎麼樣？殺了我又能改變什麼？這樣你們就能留在地上社會？牢裡嗎？

碧：阿道夫先生。

莎：阿道夫先生？啐！阿道夫，你最好別想玩文字遊戲拖延時間。一！

阿：那就開槍吧，何必數呢？因為當你們像老鼠一樣從地底下被翻起來的時候就該開這一槍了，不過你們沒有！所有勇敢的、反抗的地底人全都被送進集中營或毒氣室；當他們一天工作超過二十個小時、一天只有一塊麵包和一碗湯的時候你們在哪裡？絕大多數可悲的地底人還以為自己會過得很好，集中營不過是恐怖的謠言，等到真被送進集中營才開始抱怨這世界沒有公理、沒有上帝；就算上帝在你們耳邊咆哮，你們依然各自守著狹小的鼠窩、好看顧著你們僅有的財產！

碧：阿道夫先生，拜託您別說了！

莎：二。

阿：你們這些可悲的鼠輩只知道一邊眨著如豆般大小的眼一邊舔舐自己微

小的創痛，計較自己微薄的付出；還希望誰來給你們一點希望？卻不

知道試圖帶領你們發出聲音的領導者早死於你們自己的冷漠底下。地

底人只能淪為傭工、性玩具和肥料；一邊哀嘆自己的命運，也只哀嘆

自己的命運；對於同胞只會彼此陷害、互不搭理，甚至對立鬥爭；不

論從地下到地上、從幸福到絕望，你們從來都不知道何謂團結。怎麼

還不開槍？如果殺了我就能改變整個體制就動手呀！我一點都不介

意，因為阿道夫們會前仆後繼的出現在你們身邊，制定左右妳們生活

的決策，支配你們直到你們死在自己的冷漠底下。（停頓）三！

（莎夏一驚，扣了板機，手槍無法發射；阿道夫撿起手槍上膛。）

碧：（回應阿道夫）我們還能怎麼辦呢？

阿：那就接受吧。（扣板機，槍響。阿道夫下。除了女人們的啜泣聲外一

片靜默，許久。）

海：我說過槍該給我的。

莎：妳為什麼不告訴我怎麼操作。

海：莎夏姊姊，我知道妳仰慕阿道夫先生，怎麼可能教會妳用槍；如果妳因為個人情感開了槍，那我和碧娜姊姊該怎麼辦？

莎：妳變了，海倫娜。

海：這或許是妳教會我的。

莎：我們還能怎麼辦？回到地下？不！

（莎夏及海倫娜痛哭起來）

莎：（突然想到）抗議？對！用優雅的方法解決！我們走上街頭去抗議，讓所有人知道地下社會人也應該被重視。

（燈暗）

（節拍器規律的聲響中燈光漸亮，三位女子依著節拍器節奏進行一天抗議的生活：起床、盥洗、出門。；訴願遊行時不斷說著。）

（集結演講）

莎：請保護我們，讓地上不只有一種風景。

海：地上人、地底人平等享受陽光。

莎：請站出來聲援地底人。

碧：我們不該被犧牲。

海：請重視地底人權。

莎：地底人也有優良美德。

莎：地底人如同地上人受教育、學習地上社會法律和生活方式，如今地底人學有所成、展現特色時卻被要求重回地下，無視地底人基本權利，無視地底人意願！對地底人來說這無疑是一項暴虐的政策，請各位賢良優秀的地上人一同站出來聲援地底人！

海、碧：請各位聲援地底人。

莎、海、碧：請各位聲援地底人！

（解散、各自活動、睡覺。不停重複上述動作。重複過程中三人音量逐漸轉小，直到第四次僅剩動作和嘴型；燈光以極緩慢的速度漸暗。另一區塊燈亮，阿道夫和艾妮塔冷眼看著。）

艾：開始抗議了。

阿：那又怎麼樣？

艾：你不擔心？

阿：有什麼好擔心的。

艾：如果她們成功，她們就可以留在地上社會。

阿：嗯。

艾：並且有更多時間可以張大嘴巴不停爆料給噬血的媒體。

阿：嗯。

艾：到時候你的政治生命也隨之終結。

阿：嗯。

（停頓，艾妮塔意味深遠的看著阿道夫。）

艾：阿道夫，我不知道你什麼時候變得這麼寬宏了。

阿：怎麼說？

艾：比如說……六天後遣返。（頓）有腦子的人都知道這七天內可能會有多大的變數；半年前大家都以為地底人是野獸、未開化的人猿，政府才得以恣意妄為的……「使用」他們；不過現在大家都知道他們不過是自戰後潛藏地底的民族，「使用」上不如以往方便，甚至可以說是麻煩，偏偏總有一堆喜好自認正義的民運分子在媒體上大肆披露政府之前的暴政。

（停頓）

艾：雖然你和我同為競爭對手，但我還是應該提醒你不該讓事情變得這麼

棘手，上面的人會很不開心的，阿道夫。

阿：妳今天話真多。

艾：（微慍）我知道昨天發生什麼事。

阿：什麼事？

艾：三個女人拿著槍衝進辦公室威脅你讓他們永久留在地上。（頓）你無法決定又為了保命，所以和她們談好條件給她們七天時間爭取留下來的機會，藉由群眾和媒體的力量逼迫上層是吧。

阿：艾妮塔，妳想像力真豐富。

艾：阿道夫！盡管好整以暇地看著這場鬧劇吧，你該知道這把火遲早會燒到身上；到時候媒體會怎麼報導？最被看好的內閣總理接班人非法迫害地底人。

阿：那妳呢？

艾：（錯愕）什麼？

阿：身為教育首長卻以非人道、體罰來教育地底人。可能成為首任女內閣總理的人做這樣的事……？

艾：幼稚！我當初接到命令，必須以極其嚴厲的手段對待她們，以免地底人不服管教產生暴動。她們需要紀律，你知道嗎？那些婊子得明白她們身在何處，更重要的是明白為什麼會在這裡。只有一個辦法能讓她們明白：紀律，嚴苛的紀律。如果要對她們保持控制，這就是祕訣。

阿：這樣呀。

艾：在我看來，對政府來說是對的事情，對我來說就是對的；我無權做任何個人的思考，有任何個人的想法或情感。相反，我的職責就是毫無異議地遵守高層的命令，就算那些命令意味著用毒氣殺死千百萬地底人，我也樂意執行。相信我，這就是為什麼我不能允許自己對那些女人產生絲毫同情。

（停頓，兩人看著三個女子無聲的抗議。）

艾：（乾乾的）我總是虔誠而投入地執行任務，也始終為自己屬於地上社會的高貴人種而感到驕傲，感到有價值……。

阿：我很遺憾聽到妳這樣說。

（艾妮塔露出錯愕的表情）

阿：艾妮塔，我一直都當妳是個值得尊敬的對手。

艾：別以為多給了她們七天期限就比較仁慈！我們都在同一艘船上！出了事，誰也不會比較好過。你做過多少骯髒事！背著幾百萬的人命！

阿：我是，我確實地執行任務；但我從來沒有在心裡停止詛咒自己。（停頓）不會有誰能夠留下來；大家已經看膩這齣戲，是時候換戲碼了。

（靜默，兩人看著三個女子無聲的抗議。）

艾：阿道夫，向神祈禱這場鬧劇能順利落幕吧。

（艾妮塔忿忿走開。燈光漸暗，燈光漸暗中莎夏扯開自己的上衣、坦露胸膛。）

莎：求你們看看我們吧！我們是富有禮教的地底人！請保障我們！請聽聽我們的聲音。

（燈光厭惡似的暗掉）

（燈亮，阿道夫燈區和艾妮塔燈區亮起，眾聲喧鬧的音樂。）

艾：（驚恐的）身為教育工作者，我為我的作為感到榮耀！請各位替我的作為喝彩！也是地上社會人的榮耀！請各位替我的作為喝彩！請各位替我的作為喝彩！

（艾妮塔跌跌撞撞地走下台。阿道夫打開一根棒棒糖吃了幾口後放下；舉起手槍往自己太陽穴開了一槍，燈暗，槍聲像是無止境的回音，直到地底洞穴區燈亮。三個女子哀慟的看著地下洞穴。）

碧：我們……回家了。

海：怎麼變成這樣子、怎麼變成這樣子？

碧：除了我們之外還剩多少人活著？

海：我沒有爸爸、沒有媽媽、沒有哥哥和小小的弟弟，剩下我、只剩下我。

碧：妳還有我們。我們三個。

莎：阿道夫先生、阿道夫先生真的這樣對我們，然後可悲的自殺了。

海：自殺，讓我們活著又有什麼用？

（頓）

碧：星空，梵谷的星空。一點一點的星光和地下特有的味道和聲響。

莎：都沒有了。

碧：（堅定的）「現在」都沒有。

海：現在都沒有。

碧：今天我們談藝術。

（三人輕微地發笑，輕聲地說話。）

海：我相信在座各位必定對我們重回地下，接受文化社會陶冶的改變感到十分驚奇。

碧：如同在黑暗的甬道重新尋獲真理。

莎：這就叫重見天日嗎？

碧：（極為溫柔的）可不是嘛，到了最後……。

莎：我們還是回到大地母神的肚腹裡……。

（洞穴深處緩緩的透出光，莎夏堅定的走進洞穴深處，碧娜遲疑一會也牽著海倫娜跟著走進去。字幕『聽說重回地下的三位女子走進洞穴的深處，找到傳說中的淨地，那裡有光、有綠地和花、擁有珍貴的寶石和資源；從此，再也沒有人看過她們。』）

全劇終